When Nester joined Murdoch's coven a couple of years back, Murdoch knew they weren't beloveds. That didn't stop him from falling hard and fast for the hazel-eyed vampire, who seems to return his affection. Bringing in a donor for three-somes happens often and keeps the spice in their relationship. Murdoch is ready for the next step—family—and Nester claims to be, too. They agree to a surrogate and artificial in-semination. Except, then Murdoch ends up running late to an appointment to meet the surrogate at the facility and walks in on Nester banging the woman. His lover claims it's no big deal, but it is to Murdoch. If Nester was willing to do that with their surrogate, who else had he been involved with behind his back? Murdoch takes a step back from Nester, trying to get some perspective, angering the other vampire. A guest at the dude ranch—Malakai—offers to listen to Murdoch and of-fer advice. Murdoch finds himself extremely attracted to the gorgeous male, although his lack of scent confuses him. An unexpected accident allows Murdoch to taste Malakai's blood, revealing that not only is the male his beloved, but Ma-lakai is also an angel. Can Murdoch come to grips with the revelation—and why Malakai had hidden their connection from him—before Nester figures out a way to sabotage any hope for their future?

The Angel's Vampire
Copyright © 2021 Charlie Richards
ISBN: 978-1-4874-1960-8
Cover art by Angela Waters

Published by eXtasy Books Inc

Look for us online at:
www.eXtasybooks.com

The Angel's Vampire
A Loving Nip Book Twenty-Seven

By

Charlie Richards

DEDICATION

*We can catch a fly with honey, and we can catch even more with a
pile of horse manure.*
~Unknown

CHAPTER ONE

Trotting up the steps, Murdoch headed into the dining hall. He'd just finished untacking the nine horses he and Boyd had used on the late-morning trail ride. Boyd, his fellow wrangler and vampire, reached past him and opened the door for him.

"Thanks, man," Murdoch rumbled. Grinning at his friend, he added, "I'm starved."

Boyd nodded. "Me, too, and we have that private ride to prep for right after our afternoon ride." His brows furrowed, and his lips pinched. "Who paid for that again?"

Murdoch groaned. "Damn. I completely forgot about that." He paused in the foyer and hung his black *Stetson* on a hook, noticing Boyd doing the same with his brown one. "It's gonna make me late."

"Late for what?" Boyd asked as they both turned toward the men's room.

"Nester and I have a meeting with our surrogate this evening," Murdoch told his friend, unable to keep the grin off his face. "We're discussing whose sperm to use."

"Damn," Boyd responded as he followed Murdoch into the restroom. "You're really going ahead with that, and with Nester?"

Murdoch nodded, happiness filling him. "Yep."

As they washed the dirt and horsehair off their hands and arms, Murdoch noticed the way Boyd's brows furrowed, and the scent of his concern filled the room.

Pulling a couple of paper towels from the dispenser, Murdoch turned to face his friend. "What is it?"

Boyd cleared his throat as he dried his own hands. "It's just" — he met Murdoch's gaze squarely, revealing the worry filling his blue eyes — "Nester's not your beloved."

Murdoch shrugged. "I know, and we've discussed that. If we run into our beloved, then we'll separate amicably."

After tossing the towels in the garbage, he rested one hand on Boyd's shoulder and squeezed. In truth, Murdoch couldn't imagine how it would feel to move on from Nester. The vampire had entranced him from the moment he'd joined the coven over two years before.

Holding Boyd's gaze, Murdoch continued, "But we love each other. We're in the same place in our lives, wanting to start a family." Excitement coursed through him at the prospect of raising a child. "We've already received permission from Master Jaymes to move into a two-room suite."

"Oh, wow." Boyd's features lost some of their tension, although not all of it. "Well, I'm happy for you, man." Patting his upper arm, he added, "I sure hope it works out."

"Thanks."

Murdoch turned toward the door just as it began to open. Stepping back, he waited for whoever to enter, wondering why Boyd seemed so worried. While his friend and Nester got on about as well as oil and water, Murdoch had been in a relationship with Nester for almost two years.

Seeing the man who entered, Murdoch nearly swallowed his tongue. The guy was, in a word, stunning. He towered over Murdoch's own six-foot-one height by at least five inches. His shoulders were broad and his hips narrow, filling out his dark-blue polo shirt and chinos in all the best ways.

The man had thick, shoulder-length hair framing his aristocratic features. With the way the locks shown in the bathroom's bulbs from medium to light brown, it appeared he had highlights. Then the man pinned his intense and unique aqua-colored gaze on him, and Murdoch felt a rush of heat flood his body.

Just damn.

For an instant, Murdoch felt certain he spotted a flash of interest in the man's eyes. Then the large male turned away and headed toward a urinal. Murdoch couldn't help scoping out the man's backside, which was just as fine as his front.

Boyd jostling against his side to pass him and exit the room yanked Murdoch out of his admiration of the guy.

Swallowing the moisture that had pooled in his mouth, Murdoch followed Boyd out of the bathroom.

Once the door had closed behind them, Boyd arched one brow as he muttered, "You just eye-fucked the shit out of that guy."

Even as Murdoch squashed a fissure of guilt, he claimed, "Nester and I take donors to our bed as a third several times a month." Shrugging, he smirked as he added, "Can't blame a guy for looking at that sexy specimen. He was hawt."

Barking a laugh, Boyd asked, "You gonna approach him then?" Then he cocked his head and added, "Did you notice his lack of scent? Think he's a paranormal?"

"No, I didn't notice," Murdoch admitted.

"Too busy checking him out," Boyd replied knowingly.

Murdoch shrugged again. "Guess so, and in answer to your question, with his size, he very well could be." Since they'd reached the buffet and there were a few of their dude ranch's human guests around, Murdoch lowered his voice. "Maybe a big shifter, but why would he hide his scent?"

"Maybe he didn't realize we were a coven when he booked a vacation here," Boyd guessed. "You could ask Royce. He might know more about him since he helps in reservations."

"Naw," Murdoch said with a shake of his head. "He didn't look the type to do threesomes, and if he's hiding his scent, I'm not gonna mess with him."

For some reason, just the idea of sharing that man with Nester caused Murdoch's stomach to churn with . . . something. For the first time in over two years, he didn't want to share someone with Nester. If Murdoch were to bed that man, he would want him all to himself.

That means I have to stay far away from him.

No sense screwing up my relationship with the guy I love for someone just passing through.

With those thoughts firmly in his mind, Murdoch focused on eating his lunch.

Tapping his forefinger on the steering wheel, Murdoch drove as swiftly as he dared on the wet roads. While his vampire reflexes would have made it easy for him to control his vehicle, he had no desire to be pulled over for speeding. He was almost thirty minutes late as it was.

Fortunately, Doctor Sutherland had been understanding. He'd let Murdoch know that he'd put Nester and Lorain—the human woman who'd agreed to be their surrogate—in a room to wait. Lorain was the daughter of a woman who'd bonded with a cougar shifter when she'd been six, so she'd grown up around paranormals. Murdoch felt grateful that Doctor Sutherland had been able to connect them with her.

Murdoch spotted the lights of the clinic on his right and slowed his pick-up truck. As much as he loved his vehicle—a vintage nineteen-sixty-six *Ford F-250*—he figured he would have to get something safer for a child soon. He worried his bench seat wouldn't be conducive for a baby carrier.

Or, I could just install a middle seat belt.

Liking that idea better, Murdoch parked before cutting the engine. He hopped out of his truck, smiling happily as he locked up and shut the door. Then he headed inside.

Spotting Gary behind the reception desk, Murdoch smiled without showing his teeth. Gary was human, and Murdoch wasn't certain if he was aware of the paranormal world. As anonymity was key to their survival, Murdoch would never take that risk.

"Hi, Gary," Murdoch greeted. "How are you this evening?"

Gary grinned back at Murdoch. "Hi, Mister Sovran," he replied, addressing Murdoch with his current human surname. "I'm fine, thanks. I'll let Doctor Sutherland know you've arrived."

"Thank you." Murdoch stood a few feet back from the desk as he watched Gary make his call.

After a few seconds, Gary hung up the phone and refocused on Murdoch. "Doctor Sutherland said that Nester and Lorain are in room three. You can go on back, and he'll join you in a few minutes." Rising to his feet, Gary asked, "Do you know where that is? If not, I can show you."

Murdoch smiled while waving away the offer. "That's okay, Gary," he assured. "I know the way."

As Gary sat back down while nodding, Murdoch headed through a swinging door. He strode down the hallway, anticipation filling him. While on the drive over, Murdoch had tried to decide the best way to urge Nester to let them use his own seed. For some reason, the idea that the babe would be of Murdoch's blood felt important to him.

Maybe because of Boyd's reminder today that we're not actually beloveds. If something happened, if Nester met his beloved, I'd still be able to keep our child.

Murdoch pushed that uncharitable thought aside as he reached for the doorknob of the room Gary'd told him. Hearing a low moan from within, he paused. Then a grunt of pleasure that Murdoch knew all too well reached his ears, causing his heart to trip in his chest.

Surely not.

Turning the knob, Murdoch entered the room. His heart hammered in his chest as he took in the scene before him.

Swallowing hard, he didn't want to believe what he was seeing.

Lorain lay sprawled over the narrow patient's bed in the room. Her blouse had been spread open wide, revealing the pink lace bra that had been pushed up to her neck, displaying her full breasts. Murdoch's lover of over two years had his pants around his thighs and stood between her spread legs.

Nester pumped his hips, grunting his pleasure as he thrust his cock into Lorain's pussy over and over. With the way he leaned over her and the scents in the room, Murdoch knew Nester was feeding from Lorain.

Murdoch didn't remember gasping, but he must have made some noise of shock, for the other vampire lifted his head, licking off his fangs as he turned his attention on Murdoch. Nester grinned broadly, showing off his fangs. As he continued rutting, Nester rubbed one hand over Lorain's tit, tweaking her nipple. He had his other hand between her thighs, perhaps massaging her clit. Lorain moaned and trembled, obviously in the throes of orgasm.

"Hey, Murdoch," Nester muttered, his voice deep with his lust. "I'm almost done. Gods, her pussy feels sweet." Then he arched his back and thrust once more, letting out a throaty groan as he came.

Too shocked to respond, Murdoch just stared as Nester came down from his orgasm.

It wasn't until Nester pulled his still-hard dick from Lorain's body and, while grinning at him, said, "I'm good for the moment. Slide in and make your deposit, babe," that Murdoch managed to find his voice.

"What the fuck, Nest?" Murdoch cried, glaring at the other vampire. "What the hell is going on?"

Just as quickly, Murdoch wanted to smack himself upside the head. After all, it was obvious what was going on. Nester had decided to fuck their surrogate.

Nester responded by rolling his eyes, continuing to fondle Lorain's tit. "We wanted a baby, and Lorain's fine doing it this way, too." Shrugging, he added, "It's no big deal." Then Nester indicated the woman's still-spread thighs. "Have at her."

Shaking his head, Murdoch couldn't believe what Nester was spouting. It wasn't the fact that the vampire had gone against their decision to use artificial insemination. Instead, it was the fact that Nester had done it behind his back. If Murdoch had arrived a moment later, he probably wouldn't even have known.

Would Nester have told me? Has he fucked others without me?

Murdoch didn't know, and he was almost afraid to ask. *Almost.* Deciding to face that first, he asked, "Have there been others, Nester?" He didn't like how hoarse his voice sounded, so he swallowed and tried again. "Do you take others to our bed?"

"No," Nester denied, frowning.

Relief began to fill Murdoch, but his lover's next comment instantly destroyed it.

With a scoff, Nester stated, "I don't take others to our bed unless you're there." He rolled his hazel eyes—eyes that Murdoch had always enjoyed staring into until that moment because they were filled with such apathy. Nester revealed, "I fuck 'em in their cabin or the barn or wherever."

Murdoch wondered if a stake through his heart could possibly hurt worse. "You haven't been faithful?" he whispered the hated words.

Nester scowled, furrowing his blond brows. "What are you talking about? They're just donors." He curled his lip in an expression that actually appeared a little confused. "We're vampires. We feed from donors."

"I've never taken a donor except the ones we share together," Murdoch murmured as he took a step backward.

"Seriously?" Nester snorted. "Why not?"

Anger replaced the hurt, and Murdoch roared, "Because I was in a relationship with you!"

His shouted words finally seemed to rouse Lorain out of her post-orgasmic stupor, for she blinked open her eyes and glanced between them. Obviously spotting Murdoch's ire, she sat up, pulled her shirt around herself while pushing down her skirt. She glanced between them, and the scent of uncertainty with a hint of fear began creeping into the sex-smells that filled the room.

Nester narrowed his eyes. *"Was?"*

Did I really say that?

Yep. I did.

"I-I need time to come to grips with this," Murdoch admitted, taking a step backward. Shaking his head, he pointed at Nester. "This is not the type of relationship I thought we had. I need time to think."

"Wait a damn minute, Murdoch," Nester snapped, the other man's anger rising. "What are—"

Nester's question was cut off by the door hitting Murdoch in his back.

Stumbling forward, Murdoch caught himself as he watched Doctor Sutherland begin to enter the room. "Sorry for the wait, everyone," he began. Then he paused as he seemed to take in the sights and scents in the room. "What's going on?"

Murdoch didn't bother censoring his words as he started past the doctor. "Sorry, Doc," he growled. "Guess you won't be needed, after all. Nester decided to fuck Lorain."

Then Murdoch stalked down the hallway toward the exit, ignoring Nester shouting after him.

CHAPTER TWO

Malakai sat in a rocking chair on the porch of his rented cabin. With one foot resting against a slat of the railing, he absently rocked himself. While he appeared to be people-watching, he wasn't really seeing much.

Instead, Malakai's focus remained on Murdoch—his *stella guida*—his guiding star. Murdoch, the vampire Malakai had been assigned to befriend and assist, was his reason for being. Unfortunately, Murdoch was also in a committed relationship with another.

As an angel, Malakai had not only the heightened abilities most valued by paranormals—increased strength, hearing, sight, agility, and more—but he had another unique gift. If the person felt strongly enough about something, Malakai could read their thoughts.

And Murdoch was definitely attracted to me. Not only did his arousal give him away, but his thoughts of me did, too.

But he's living with another. Planning a child with another.

Malakai sighed deeply, his heart aching with that knowledge. When he'd realized he was being sent to a vampire coven, he'd not only cloaked his true form—his wings and aura—hiding it from everyone, but he'd suppressed his scent, as well. Malakai hadn't wanted to be approached by a vampire with the prospect of becoming a donor, seeing as being an angel, he didn't have a sex drive until he met his *stella guida*.

Little did I know.

He knew Murdoch hadn't recognized him as his beloved,

attraction or not. It had been so very tempting to reveal his scent when he'd locked eyes on his vampire in that bathroom. Except, with his heightened hearing, he'd heard all about how Murdoch loved another and planned to use a surrogate to have a child with him.

Confused, with hurt panging through his heart, Malakai closed his eyes and sought out his creator — an ancient being many humans would liken to the god they chose to follow. Long ago, at the dawn of humans and paranormals, his creator had called angels into being to aid in keeping the emotional and spiritual balance between those in this realm.

Considering Malakai's last assignment had been to help a husband and three young children process the emotional turmoil caused by the cheating and vocally abusive now-ex-wife, Malakai figured more angels needed to get off their butts and work a little bit harder.

I feel your turmoil, Malakai.

Upon hearing his creator's voice in his head, Malakai embraced the warmth of his maker's presence. *I have met Murdoch, the vampire.*

And?

Wincing, even with his eyes closed, Malakai shared his troubles. *He is my* stella guida, *but he is already in a relationship. He loves another.*

You know soul mates trump everything. His creator reminded Malakai of a fundamental truth held by all paranormals. *But I see you hid yourself from him.*

Malakai sensed his creator's disappointment, and shame curdled in his gut. *I worried about his reaction. He plans to have a child with his partner.*

Do you not care for the idea of raising a vampire child with your stella guida?

Malakai gasped, nearly opening his eyes in shock. He just managed to stay the reaction, knowing it would sever his link with his creator. Instinctively, he shook his head.

I would be honored to raise a child with Murdoch. Malakai couldn't get the counter thought through their mental link quickly enough. Knowing he needed to reveal his greatest fear, he shared his troubles with his creator. *What if he comes to resent me because I took him away from the vampire he's loved for over two years?*

You were sent to meet Murdoch. Surely you can see that the timing is for a reason. His creator's reassuring voice carried through Malakai's mind. *Talk to your vampire.*

With that, Malakai felt the calming presence of his creator recede from him. Still, he whispered, "Yes, Creator."

When Malakai opened his eyes, he felt a wealth of new purpose surfacing within him. As he sat there watching the sun set, he tried to come up with some kind of plan. As an angel, there were several things to consider.

Malakai knew that to begin their bond, Murdoch had to choose him. He also knew that a vampire would do that without thought because of one simple fact—once a vampire scented or tasted their beloved, any other blood would begin to taste sour. In order for a vampire to live, they needed their beloved.

I refuse to trap him that way. I'll leave my scent blocked until we have a chance to get to know each other. If my stella guida *is truly happy, then I'll fulfill my duties and move on. I can always keep an eye on him over the years. I am eternal, after all.*

With that decision made, Malakai rose and headed into the cabin to prepare for bed. He would seek out Murdoch the following day.

Considering Murdoch was a wrangler, Malakai decided to sign up for a trail ride. He jotted his name on the list, indicating in the blank line under special considerations that he was six-foot-six and over two-hundred-fifty pounds. While Malakai had never weighed himself, he figured that was something those gathering mounts would need to know.

Then Malakai headed into the dining hall. He grabbed three pre-made sausage breakfast burritos, picante sauce, and a cup of English breakfast tea. Then he relaxed in a chair in the corner.

Malakai had his glamour firmly in place, hiding his celestial light — an aura that would have humans quickly falling at their feet before him — as well as his wings. His feathered appendages were still there, however. If anyone accidentally touched them, they would dismiss it as a brush of silk against their skin, but Malakai was protective of his wings. He preferred they remain out of anyone's reach.

As Malakai ate, he roved his attention over the comings and goings. He knew he was looking for Murdoch, but he couldn't help himself, either. Knowing the vampire was his *stella guida* created a wave of urgings that Malakai had never before experienced, and he wasn't certain what to make of them.

Hopefully, I'll be able to control myself when I see him again.

After eating, Malakai headed toward the exit. He supposed it was for the best that he hadn't seen his star there. One night away from him and he was already missing him, even though they hadn't said a word to each other. As Malakai had been watching the door, he'd begun thinking about all the things he wanted to do to the vampire.

Malakai wanted to stare into Murdoch's gorgeous, pale-blue eyes once more. He wanted to push the man's slightly shaggy, dark-auburn hair away from his face, to tuck a few strands behind his ear, and cradle his jaw.

What will his hair feel like? I bet it's soft. Will I be able to feel a bit of scruff, a five-o-clock shadow, I believe it's called?

As an angel, Malakai didn't grow facial hair. It seemed that none of their kind did. Angels had little body hair, even on their groin. Perhaps that was why the idea of Murdoch having a pelt of chest hair appealed to him.

"Hey, watch it."

The blond vampire's snarled words snapped Malakai's attention back to the here and now. He barely twisted sideways enough to avoid the shorter, slender male who was barreling up the middle of the dining hall's porch stairs as if he owned the space. Glancing over his shoulder, Malakai spotted the anger glittering in the guy's hazel eyes.

The vampire's thoughts flittered through his mind.

Big bastard thinks he owns the road. Gods, I'd love to take him down a notch. Maybe after I find Murdoch.

Malakai paused at the bottom of the steps, continuing to stare at the blond vampire even as he began disappearing into the dining hall. The male's thoughts continued to reach him for a couple of heartbeats.

Can't believe how Murdoch's acting. As if I've done something wrong. When I catch up with him, I'm —

The thoughts drifted away, telling Malakai the man was too far out of range. As tempting as it was to follow the vampire to discover more of the man's plans, he had somewhere to be instead. Besides, if he managed to figure out a way to stay near Murdoch's side, he could protect him from whatever the other vampire had been ranting about.

Malakai turned and headed toward the staging area for the trail rides. He knew the vampire coven owned several thousand acres and raised Angus beef. They ran the guest ranch as a way to secretly garner blood donors.

The twelve-stall barn housed a number of the mounts, while the rest were kept in paddocks close by. There were two rows of hitching posts where up to ten horses could be tied.

As Malakai approached the area, he spotted the big blond who'd been in the restroom with Murdoch the prior day — Boyd. The vampire was busy tacking up a large horse at the end that appeared to be half-draft. When a second vampire appeared from the barn, leading a smaller black horse, Malakai recognized him as Royce, the vampire who'd checked him into the ranch the prior morning.

To Malakai's disappointment, Murdoch was nowhere to be seen. Knowing it would appear odd if he just walked away when he'd already signed up for the ride, he continued toward the area. Eight other horses were already saddled and ready, and three obvious groups of four were clustered together talking — one clearly a family, parents and two kids — while the other was a group of women. When those four peered Malakai's way, he shut off his gift of reading people's thoughts because some of their ideas made him distinctly uncomfortable.

Steering clear of them, Malakai stopped beside Boyd. He smiled at the vampire. "Hi, there," he greeted softly, catching the male's attention. "I'm going to guess that this big fella is mine."

Boyd smiled, his blue eyes dancing with amusement as he looked Malakai up and down. "You'd be right, and it's a she, actually." He held out his hand. "I'm Boyd."

"Malakai," he offered, taking the vampire's hand. "Nice to meet you." Turning his attention to the big horse standing quietly at the hitching post, he asked, "And who's this lovely girl?"

"This is Shamrock. Named because the star on her forehead kinda looks like one," Boyd told him with a smile. "My boss's stallion got loose and bred one of our quarter horses, and she was the result." He patted the big animal's neck while smiling fondly. "She's a good girl."

After a couple more moments sharing information about Shamrock, Boyd headed toward Royce. The pair of wranglers went through a spiel about safety as well as riding instructions. Then they assisted those who needed it before mounting their own horses and leading them out of the yard.

Malakai had spent centuries on horseback, and he found

the ride soothing. The area they traveled through was gorgeous, but his mind kept drifting to Murdoch.

Where was he, and why wasn't he there?

When the ride finished, Malakai offered to assist the wranglers. After they'd exchanged glances and offered the *you don't have to* placation, they accepted his aid.

As soon as the others had wandered away, Malakai could no longer contain his curiosity. "Doesn't Murdock normally do this, Boyd?" Upon seeing the way Boyd's eyes narrowed, he quickly added, "I overheard a few of your words in the restroom yesterday."

Boyd nodded once before slowly replying, "Murdoch's not feeling well, so he took a day."

Malakai scented the lie. He also caught the vampire's fleeting thought.

Why is this guy asking about Murdoch? Did he see him checking him out in the restroom and plans to kick his ass for it?

While it saddened Malakai that Boyd would immediately think ill of him due to his size, he ignored that. Instead, he offered Boyd a crooked smile and commented, "It's tough for a vampire to get sick. Was he injured somehow and needs a day to recover?" Just the idea that his *stella guida* was hurt caused his instincts to scream for him to find Murdoch as swiftly as possible.

Royce paused at Boyd's side. With narrowed eyes, he inhaled deeply. "What are you?" he demanded softly. "What's your interest in Murdoch?"

For just an instant, Malakai released his glamour, giving the pair of vampires a fleeting glance of his wings and aura. He watched their eyes widen, and the scent of arousal teased his senses. Taking a step backward, he lifted his hands in placation.

"Well, fuck me," Boyd whispered before clearing his throat and shaking his head, obviously clearing it of the lustful thoughts that had suddenly filled it. When he focused on Malakai again, Boyd chuckled. "With mojo like that, no wonder you hide."

Malakai smiled. "Exactly." Then he sighed. "And I really just wanted to touch base with Murdoch. Make certain everything's okay. Can you help me?"

With bated breath, Malakai waited for the vampires to make a decision. Even though, with a touch to each of them, he could have urged them to help, he wanted them to do it of their own free will. After all, these were Murdoch's friends. Malakai wanted to start things off on the right foot.

CHAPTER THREE

M urdoch knew he couldn't put off facing Nester forever. As good as Boyd was to allow him to sleep on his suite's sofa, he knew that, eventually, his partner would figure out where to look for him. After all, Boyd had warned him that Nester had been asking around for him.

Probably only because Boyd and Nester had never gotten along had saved Murdoch from Nester pounding on Boyd's door for the last two days. Hell, the pair had practically been ordered to stay away from each other by Second Gypsum. That had been a year and a half before when they'd come to blows over an argument that neither would share with Murdoch, and they still avoided each other.

Damn. Maybe that should have been a sign.

Had Boyd spotted Nester seducing someone behind my back? But why hadn't Boyd ever said anything?

Right. Because my buddy knew I was head-over-heels in love with the guy.

The image of Nester shagging Lorain flashed through his mind, and he barely managed to keep down the cup of coffee he'd just finished.

Unable to stand staring at the four walls of Boyd's front room a second longer, Murdoch rose to his feet. He grabbed his hat from the rack and eased out of the room. The coven house was mostly quiet as he moved through the halls. Most everyone else would be out working.

Guilt churned in Murdoch's gut. He shouldn't be shirking his duties, but he just hadn't been able to face anyone. He still didn't want to.

Except, right then, Master Jaymes Martinez turned the corner before him, and Murdoch froze, feeling like a kid who'd just been caught with his hand in the cookie jar.

Jaymes strode toward him, arching one dark brow. "So, you're done hiding in Boyd's room. Good." Smirking, he tipped his chin back the way he'd been coming. "I'm glad. I was just coming to get you. Join me in my office, Murdoch."

When Jaymes pivoted and strode away from Murdoch, he followed. The hairs on the back of his neck stood on end, and he wondered how much trouble he was in. Had Nester said something to their master about him?

Opening his office door, Jaymes preceded Murdoch inside. He closed the door behind them. Instead of sitting behind his desk, he moved to a sofa where Paul—Jaymes's human beloved—already sat. Jaymes settled beside his lover, cradled his neck, and pressed a kiss to his lips.

Jaymes returned his focus to Murdoch, and Paul did the same.

To his surprise, Paul smiled at him and waved toward a nearby chair. "Have a seat, Murdoch." The human bounced to his feet and headed toward the sideboard. "Can I get you a drink? Coffee? Beer?" A troubled expression creased his brows. "Something stronger?"

"Uh, c-coffee's fine," Murdoch managed to reply. "Thanks."

"I know why you've been hiding in Boyd's suite," Paul told him as he poured a rich dark brew into a mug, surprising Murdoch that the human seemed to be taking the lead. "And, I have to say, I don't blame you at all." Putting down the carafe, he brought the mug to him. "Black, right?"

Murdoch nodded as he took the mug. "Yes, thank you." Then he frowned as he watched Paul return to his seat beside Master Jaymes, who immediately wrapped his arm around the slender human. Murdoch did his best to ignore the niggle of jealousy he felt upon seeing the bonded couple's happiness at just being close to each other. "Um. H-How?"

Master Jaymes shook his head as a small smile curved his lips. "Murdoch. How long have you been with me?" It seemed to be a rhetorical question, for the master kept talking. "I'm aware of just about everything that goes on in my coven." With a deep sigh, Jaymes admitted, "Although, I admit I did not know that you were unaware that Nester took donors aside from the ones you shared. Ever since he joined us, he's always seemed to have a high lust for blood."

"Gods, did everyone know but me?" Murdoch whispered before taking a sip of his coffee.

Jaymes shook his head. "No, Nester was discreet."

"I'm actually the one who stumbled upon him just as he was finishing up with some lady here on vacation with a few of her friends," Paul admitted, grimacing. "I questioned him, but I'm human. I wouldn't have been able to scent his lies." His cheeks darkened with embarrassment. "And I guess it never occurred to me that one of our vampires would ever lie to me, considering my position here."

While Paul was young — he'd bonded with Jaymes several years before when he was just eighteen — the man had taken to his duties as the beloved of the master with ease. He'd taken courses online, teaching him how to help run the business. He'd watched training videos for foal handling and picked it up swiftly, and he was now one of the best at the ranch for imprinting a newborn.

Hell, the foals practically followed him around anytime he was with them, ignoring their mothers unless they were hungry.

"Believe me," Jaymes stated on a growl. "I will be speaking with Nester about lying to my beloved." Then his expression turned concerned. "But I wanted to speak with you first. Do

19

you intend to continue seeing him, or should I speak with Gypsum about finding you alternate accommodations?"

And that's the crux of the problem, isn't it?

As a vampire, Murdoch understood the drive to find a donor and enjoy their blood. Was he willing to accept an open relationship with Nester? Did he love him that much?

"I-I don't know," Murdoch admitted, cradling his coffee mug between his knees. "I know he's not my beloved. I wish he'd been honest with me about his needs. I—" Murdoch sighed deeply before shrugging his shoulders helplessly. "I don't know."

Jaymes nodded. "I suspected as much. So, please don't take this assignment as if it's a punishment. It's not." As he spoke, he lifted his hand in placation. "You need time to decide what you want to do, and I need the fences on the west end of the property checked. It's rugged terrain and will take you several days on horseback."

"Fence checking?" Murdoch hadn't done that in years, but he suddenly found it appealing. The weather was fair that week. They weren't expecting rain, so he could spend the evenings enjoying the stars. He could get away and figure out his shit. "I'd be happy to. Which pack horse should I take?"

After Jaymes named a pack horse, he added, "If there's a project too big for you to handle alone, pin the GPS location on your phone's map with a note of what's needed, and I'll send a team to address it."

Nodding, Murdoch felt better than he had in days. "Thank you for understanding. I'll let you know what I've decided upon my return." Then he rose to his feet, already mentally cataloging the supplies he would need.

Murdoch guessed it would take at least three days to make the loop that he knew he would need to travel in order to check everything on their ranch's western edge. He appreciated that his master had already been thinking of ways to help him. It reinforced his respect for the vampire.

Jaymes and Paul both rose, too. "After tacking up your mounts, go to Vaughn," he instructed. "He'll have your food for the trip ready." Slinging his arm around Paul's shoulder, Jaymes told him, "Mathe has Nester with him prepping tonight's chuckwagon dinner, so you won't be at risk of running into him."

"Thank you, Master," Murdoch replied, dipping his head in a grateful nod. "I appreciate it."

Paul eased out of Jaymes's hold and crossed to him. "Good luck," he offered before wrapping Murdoch in an oh-so-brief hug. "We'll back whatever you decide."

Murdoch nodded, his voice turning thick. "Thank you," he whispered again. Then he started toward the door.

Just as Murdoch opened it, Master Jaymes called, "And Murdoch." Peering over his shoulder at his coven master, he saw the head vampire's reassuring smile. "We'll get you through this."

Dipping his chin in a nod, Murdoch didn't know what else to say. Plus, getting his tongue to work at that point would have been damn near impossible. Hurrying from the room, Murdoch turned toward his own suite.

As Murdoch entered the space he'd shared with Nester for almost two years, a sense of sadness flowed over him. He took in the dirty laundry draped over the back of the sofa and the dirty dishes on the coffee table. Shaking his head, he hurried into the bedroom, finding it in an answering state with clothes on the floor and the bed covers rumpled.

Murdoch only scented Nester, which reminded him of how the man had kept his secret for so long. Just as his lover had said, he'd never brought a donor to their bed. Did that mean something?

Shaking his head, Murdoch quickly grabbed a backpack from the closet before crossing to his dresser. He resisted the urge to straighten up the place. As he placed several changes of clothes into the bag, he realized how cleaning had always fallen on him.

Gods, he's sort of a slob, isn't he?

Wondering how he'd never noticed that before, he quickly finished gathering everything he would need for a short camping trip. He knew the outdoor supplies needed would be in the storage room downstairs—tarps, tents, sleeping bags, and more. Every vampire had access to them, and when they returned them, they were required to make certain they were clean and ready to be used again.

Downstairs, Murdoch picked out a tarp and sleeping bag, forgoing the tent. He chose a package containing waterproof matches and other fire-starting odds and ends. Finally, he chose a waterproof duster in his size and headed out of the house.

Murdoch spotted a number of guests, and he smiled and waved at each. Instead of heading to the barn housing the horses the guests used, he strode to a barn further away. There were younger mounts inside—those still in training. He figured it was as good a time as any to put some miles on one.

After choosing a dark-bay gelding with soft eyes—Duke—Murdoch tied him to a hitching post outside the barn and saddled him. He rested the bridle over the saddle's horn for later. Then he chose the mule—Hazel—that his master had offered for a pack animal. Hazel was named for his color—a deep, burnt-orange shade. He was also experienced, so if Duke did something stupid, his pack-mule wouldn't get upset.

Once Murdoch had his animals in order, he headed to the dining hall. Instead of using the main entrance, he went in through the back. True to his master's words, their coven's chef—Vaughn—had a bulging set of saddlebags ready.

After Vaughn wished him a safe trip, he returned to his work.

As Murdoch headed back to his horse, Boyd jogged up to him. "Hey, man. It's great to see you out and about." His buddy smiled at him. Then the other vampire must have noticed Duke and Hazel. "Where ya goin'?"

Murdoch told Boyd of his conversation with Master Jaymes as he slung his saddlebag into place behind his saddle. "I'll be back in a few days." He tapped his noggin. "Get my head on straight."

Boyd chuckled and patted his shoulder. "Not too straight, I hope," he said with a wink.

Chuckling, Murdoch nodded. "Right." Most of the vampires in their coven were bisexual, which worked out well since their ranch catered to just as many men as women. Murdoch swung into the saddle before offering, "See you in a few days."

"Stay safe," Boyd replied with a wave.

Murdoch waved back and started on his way, walking toward a pasture he would need to cross to reach a trail leading to the western edge of the ranch.

To Murdoch's surprise, he found he was looking forward to his time away from the ranch . . . and Nester.

CHAPTER FOUR

Malakai appreciated Boyd's heads up as well as the use of Shamrock. While the saddlebag of foodstuffs had been a thoughtful touch, he hadn't needed it. He hadn't bothered to share that he could have used magick to create whatever food he and Murdoch would need.

No need to tell him more about angels than I have to, yet.

Boyd had shown him on a map on his phone where Murdoch would be. While he appreciated the information, he could have just followed his *stella guida*'s alluring scent. Due to the lack of wind, coupled with him being only an hour behind his vampire, he enjoyed the way his smell lingered in the air.

Delicious.

For the first time in his life, Malakai experienced the discomfort of riding a horse with an erection. Even that didn't make him soften, however. His anticipation regarding seeing Murdoch again after nearly three days kept him hard.

Considering Murdoch was leading a pack-mule, Malakai figured he was moving faster than his vampire. That didn't leave him with much time to come up with a reason for why he was out there. Malakai didn't want to out and out lie to his star, but he didn't want to share what they were to each other, yet, either.

Malakai needed to assess Murdoch's state of mind. Boyd had explained that his *stella guida* was feeling betrayed by Nester due to his actions. His vampire might not be ready to jump into anything new, even if he did decide to leave the other man.

I'll give him all the time he needs before asking him to choose me.

Malakai just hoped a few days riding fence together would be enough. In fact, he hoped Murdoch would accept his offer to travel with him at all. His vampire could decide he was just a nosey guest and send him back to the ranch.

Hmmm . . . I need to think of something because his scent is strengthening.

I can do this. I have to.

As Malakai's horse crested the rise, he realized he would have to do that in a hurry. He spotted Murdoch winding his way along the narrow trail quite a ways below him. Drawing his horse to a stop, Malakai took a moment to admire his *stella guida.*

I'm truly blessed.

Murdoch was built long and lean, his muscular frame moving easily and confidently with the horse beneath him. His black hat hid his dark-auburn hair, but Malakai still recalled his urge to run his fingers through it. The black duster stretched over his shoulders, falling halfway down his legs, hiding much from Malakai's view, but he didn't need to see it again to remember it from their brief interaction in the bathroom.

Right. As if we interacted. I look forward to changing that.

Malakai waited until Murdoch had almost reached the bottom before urging Shamrock forward. As his horse's long walking stride ate up the distance, he continued to keep an eye on his vampire. He knew the second the equines realized another was behind him, and he felt grateful he'd waited.

While the mule just flicked its ears to listen behind it while raising its head a bit in obvious acknowledgment, the bay squirted forward in alarm. The mule immediately kept pace, jogging to keep up. Murdoch reined in the bay after a couple of strides. It took a minute more to calm the animal's prancing.

By then, Murdoch had half-turned the bay around, and the vampire's focus lifted to Malakai. As he continued closer, he spotted the questioning look in Murdoch's expression. The vampire even glanced up behind him as if searching for someone — maybe the rest of a trail riding group.

"Hi, Murdoch," Malakai greeted, unable to help but smile at his handsome *stella guida*. "I'm glad I waited to start down until you were at the bottom. Is he a young one?"

Holy shit! What is he doing out here?

Murdoch's thoughts reached Malakai just before the vampire found his tongue. "Yeah." Cocking his head, he added, "This gelding is only three. Still needs a lot of miles." Then he glanced toward the rise again before refocusing on Malakai. "Did you get lost from your trail group, sir? I can tie up my mule and show you back part way."

Shaking his head, Malakai admitted, "I asked Boyd where you were going, and he let me borrow Shamrock for a few days." He touched his chest and added, "I'm Malakai, by the way."

Okay. What the hell? Why would Boyd send a guest that he knows I have the hots for out here after me? Especially at a time like this?

While Murdoch had plenty of thoughts running through his head, he seemed to be having trouble deciding what to actually say.

"Uh, I don't, um, understand why he'd do that," Murdoch finally stuttered out uncertainly.

Malakai shrugged one shoulder before he pointed in the direction Murdoch had been heading. "I hear you're on fence duty for the next few days." There hadn't been a question in Murdoch's comment, so Malakai figured he didn't have to try to make something up. "I look forward to seeing more of your coven's gorgeous ranch."

"Coven?" Murdoch whispered, his eyes widening. "You know of us."

Malakai nodded as he started his horse around Murdoch's, hoping he would begin to follow. To his pleasure, his *stella guida* did. Murdoch urged his gelding to fall in step with his big mare, and the mule followed along docilely.

"How do you know of us?" Murdoch demanded with narrowed eyes. "What are you?"

Sexy fucker or not, if he's a danger, I'll have to take him out.

Unable to help himself, Malakai cracked a smile upon hearing Murdoch's thoughts. As if his vampire could take out an angel. Of course, he wouldn't mind wrestling with his gorgeous man.

"Well?"

Upon hearing Murdoch's forcefulness, Malakai pushed away his lustful thoughts. "I'm a paranormal as well," he hedged slowly. "So when I realized this dude ranch was run by a vampire coven, I suppressed my scent, so no one would find the smell of my blood alluring."

"Why?"

At least Murdoch wasn't sending him away.

Malakai scoffed softly as he admitted, "Because my kind are unique in the fact that we don't feel arousal until we meet our soul mate." Smiling wryly, he told the vampire, "I didn't want to get involved in anything . . . awkward."

Murdoch nodded once, even as a bit of disappointment filled his scent. "Okay. I suppose I can understand that." Then he frowned and asked, "So why did Boyd send you out here with me? Why'd you come here?"

Gods, I hope you're not a danger to us, even if I won't be able to talk you into bed.

Fuck! I shouldn't be thinking like that unless I've made a decision about Nester. I refuse to be like him.

"So I can keep you company," Malakai told him. Then he gave his guiding star a small smile. "And to offer the ear and support of a stranger, if you so desire it. I've heard it said that it's easier to discuss problems with strangers. Hence the popularity of bartenders and psychologists."

To Malakai's relief, Murdoch scoffed. "You're here on vacation. Surely you don't want to hear some random vampire's problems."

It was on the tip of Malakai's tongue to tell Murdoch that he was no random vampire, but he fought the urge back. Instead, he shrugged and told him, "I have nothing else going on."

Murdoch sighed deeply. When he glanced at Malakai, his brows were furrowed. "I should really send you back. You didn't sign up for riding fence and sleeping on the ground." He frowned more deeply. "I don't even have a sleeping bag for you."

Malakai patted the saddlebag behind him. "I have everything I need." Even if he didn't have a sleeping bag in there, he could magick one up easily enough.

I suppose I could use the company. Plus, how am I supposed to figure out if he's a danger to my coven if I send him away?

"Okay." Murdoch glanced at him once more. "I plan to be doing a lot of trotting. Do you ride regularly? I don't want you to end up hurting."

Smiling, pleased to have won the right to ride by his *stella guida's* side, Malakai admitted, "I ride more than I sit in a car."

It was true, too. There were no vehicles in his creator's realm. Although, while there were mounts and everyone knew how to ride, most angels flew from one place to another.

"So, Malakai, what brought you to vacation at our dude ranch?" Murdoch asked as he urged his gelding to pick up a trot.

Malakai easily kept pace as he decided on how to answer. "I would like to hold off on explaining that until we know each other better," he decided to go with because he couldn't tell his vampire the truth without revealing his nature.

"Fair enough," Murdoch replied.

Thinking quickly, Malakai tried to decide how to steer the conversation back to Murdoch and his troubles. "I overheard you and Boyd in the restroom that day we bumped into each other." Even as he spotted the tightening of Murdoch's jaw, he forged ahead. "You were going to have a baby with your partner. Did that fall through?"

"Yes," Murdoch replied through gritted teeth.

"I'm sorry."

Malakai was, too. He wanted his *stella guida* happy above all else — even if that meant him being with another.

Uncertain how to ask what had happened, Malakai allowed the silence to lengthen. Boyd had only shared that Murdoch's lover had betrayed him in some way, hurting him deeply, but he hadn't shared particulars. Fortunately, the silence didn't feel oppressive, and he enjoyed the scenery. It changed from rolling hills to steep inclines and descents and back again. Malakai didn't know where they were going, and to him, it didn't matter. He just appreciated being by the side of his guiding star.

Finally, Murdoch broke the silence. "I've been in a relationship with Nester for over two years." The vampire was glaring at the terrain ahead as he continued, "I thought we were monogamous except for when we decided to share a donor. I was, at least."

While Malakai would rather not hear about Murdoch having sex with others, he had said he would listen. A man of his word, he nodded once. "But he was not?"

Murdoch shook his head sharply. "No. I found that out by walking in on him fucking our surrogate."

Malakai couldn't help but whisper, "By the creator, I'm so very sorry."

The scent of pain mixed with humiliation and indignation rolling off his *stella guida* sent a wave of protectiveness through Malakai. The desire to find this Nester character and hand him his head burned through him. As an angel, anger wasn't something he normally felt, but he did right then.

Grunting, Murdoch told him, "He claimed it was no big deal. I asked him if he took other donors to our bed other than the ones we shared." The bark of laughter Murdoch let out was cold and harsh. "He had the audacity to tell me that he didn't take them to our bed. He fucked them elsewhere."

It suddenly hit Malakai as to why he'd been sent to Murdoch at that time—to repair his *stella guida's* shattered trust. As the vampire's beloved, Malakai would never be able to stray. He would put the other man's needs above his own in all things.

Just as Malakai prepared to remove his glamour and scent suppression spells, Murdoch's next words stopped him.

"So, I'm out here trying to decide if I love Nester enough to accept his lust for donors and heightened need for blood."

Malakai clamped down on his desire to growl. He desperately wanted to declare that Murdoch was his, but he couldn't. Even in pain, his vampire spoke of loving another.

I have to wait until he's ready to choose me, instead.

CHAPTER FIVE

Murdoch spotted so many emotions flickering across Malakai's features that he couldn't quite keep up. The man seemed upset on his behalf, but there was something more there, too. He just wasn't certain what.

The fact that Malakai gave off no scent frustrated the hell out of him. Add in the information that whatever the hell Malakai was, he couldn't get aroused unless it was his beloved, made him feel a little like a creep. Had he not been struggling with his relationship with Nester, Murdoch knew he would have been trying to get into Malakai's pants something fierce.

What the hell kind of paranormal doesn't have a sex drive?

Murdoch couldn't think of any. Even demons had a sex drive, and they were the only ones he could think of that could use magick to suppress their scent. Drawing a blank frustrated the hell out of him.

"So, uh, what do you think I should do?" Murdoch blurted out, for want of something to say.

Malakai appeared startled. His unique aqua-colored eyes widened, and he almost reminded Murdoch of a deer caught in the headlights. He even swallowed so hard his Adam's apple bobbed.

For the briefest of seconds, Murdoch saw something that reminded him of hunger, desire even, cross Malakai's features. Then the look was gone. Plus, he'd said that he couldn't get aroused, so that couldn't have been right.

Clearing his throat, Malakai sounded a little rough as he mused, "I suppose you're asking yourself if you love Nester enough to accept that you can't keep him all to yourself." His brows furrowed, and his expression turned troubled. "Would accepting that the other vampire would never truly be all yours be something that you could live with? Or would you come to resent him?"

Murdoch gave that the consideration it was due. Would he come to resent Nester?

Or do I already? I'm definitely mad as hell at him. Lying cheating asshole.

On the other hand—"We never verbally outlined our relationship," Murdoch murmured, trying to sort through his myriad of feelings. Hurt and betrayal were definitely the biggest ones, but did he have a right to feel them? "We moved in together, claiming to love each other. But we're not beloveds, and we both know that."

There was a reason vampires normally stayed single until meeting their beloveds. Or if they did come together, it was purely platonic in the emotions department so they could have a child or two. Then once their kid was old enough to understand—assuming neither had found their beloved—they separated and co-parented as friends.

"I think I made a horrible, horrible mistake," Murdoch whispered, shaking his head. "I wanted a relationship and went about it the wrong way."

"Did Nester say he loved you, too?"

Murdoch peered Malakai's way, surprised by the slight growl in his voice when he spoke Nester's name.

Huh. What does that mean?

"Yeah. He tells me all the time." Reaching a narrow ravine, Murdoch paused his gelding. As he sought out a safe place to cross, a thought hit him. "Of course, it's only after I've said it first."

Did that mean something?

With a mental sigh, Murdoch wondered if he stopped saying it, would either of them say it again?

Murdoch had no idea.

Spotting a narrow spot that the horses could easily pop over, Murdoch headed that way. It took a little urging, but he managed to get Duke to jump the opening. He landed on the other side and began to climb up, pleased to note that Hazel followed right along.

When Malakai moved Shamrock into position to jump it, Murdoch realized he should have checked that the other man was comfortable doing that. Just as he opened his mouth, the big mare made the leap. Watching Malakai's big frame, Murdoch admired how easy he made the movement look.

Wait. Did I see something sparkling behind him?

Murdoch blinked, and the odd ripple effect around Malakai's shoulders was gone.

Weird.

"You were serious when you said you rode often," Murdoch commented, impressed that the big man didn't seem at all fazed by the terrain they traveled through. He started them up the opposite side of the ravine. "Where did you grow up? How old are you?"

Being a paranormal, Murdoch didn't think that was too much to ask.

"I—" Malakai paused and frowned. "I don't know how old I am, and I didn't grow up around here . . . or at all."

Confused at the answer, Murdoch frowned at the larger male. "What's that supposed to mean?"

Malakai hesitated, obviously uncertain what or how to share . . . something. Then he pointed. "Is that the fence line we're following?"

"It is." Murdoch knew a deferral when he heard one.

Except Malakai continued to point into the distance. "There's a break there."

Trying to see what Malakai was referring to, Murdoch stared at the fence line. He didn't see it, but some of the fence was hidden behind bushes as well as a few trees. If there was indeed a break, he needed to check it out to see if he could fix it with the supplies he'd brought.

"Okay," Murdoch conceded. "Let's check it out." Before urging Duke forward, he pointed at Malakai. "Don't think I won't revisit this topic."

Malakai nodded once, although his expression appeared pensive.

Wondering why that would be, Murdoch focused on getting to where Malakai had indicated. After five minutes of careful navigation over the rocky terrain, he reached the fence. He followed along it until he spotted that there was indeed a break.

Murdoch looked over his shoulder at where they'd been talking at the top of the ridge. "Damn," he muttered. "You must have amazing eyesight."

Malakai smirked. "It is exceptional."

Chuckling, Murdoch shook his head. He swung off Duke's back and dropped the reins. One of the first things they taught a youngster was how to ground tie. Unless something crazy happened, his gelding wouldn't move more than a few feet.

Murdoch crossed to the fence and inspected the gap. A tree branch had fallen during some storm, right onto one of the posts. It has been heavy enough to snap the post, laying the barbed wire fence on the ground.

Humming, Murdoch lifted a branch here and there, trying to decide if he would need to sink a whole new post. "You know, I think I can repair this," he decided, turning to face Malakai. "If you don't mind giving me a hand."

Malakai swung off of Shamrock, landing lightly on the ground. With a smile, he told him, "I'm at your disposal."

"Have you ever fixed a fence before?" Murdoch asked curiously. The man was great on a horse, so maybe somewhere back in however long he'd lived, he'd worked a ranch before.

Shaking his head, Malakai admitted, "That I have not

done." He crossed to him as he added, "But if you tell me what to do, I'll do my best."

Even as that answer surprised him, Murdoch nodded. "Okay. Gloves first when working with barbed wire." He returned to Duke to pull out his own pair. "Do you have any?"

"I believe so," Malakai replied, eyeing the thick, cow-hide working gloves Murdoch was pulling on.

When Malakai moved toward his own saddlebags, Murdoch went to Hazel. He opened a side bag and searched for what he needed—wire cutters, hammer and nails, pliers, and a small coil of barbed wire which he could use to fill a gap.

Just as Murdoch started toward the fence, he heard Malakai mutter something under his breath. He was about to ask what he'd said when a strange tingle tickled his skin. Feeling the hairs on his nape stand on end, he cocked his head.

Odd.

Murdoch shrugged off the sensation in favor of getting to work. Hopefully, getting sweaty and dirty would help distract him from the sexy man who'd ended up accompanying him. Of course, as he watched Malakai saunter toward him, tugging on a pair of gloves that appeared similar to his own, Murdoch didn't think anything could distract him from the guy's handsomeness.

"Okay." Murdoch cleared his throat, refocusing on the task at hand. "I'm going to cut the wire so we can pull it from beneath the downed tree limb, then off the post." He began putting deed to word. "Then we'll trim the tree branches out of the way so we can string up a temporary fence between those two other posts." As Murdoch used the wire cutters to snip the downed lines, he added, "And I'll ping this location so my coven can bring in the necessary supplies to implement a long-term fix."

"All right."

Murdoch paused before cutting the last wire to peer over his shoulder at Malakai. He noticed the interested way the big sexy fucker watched what he was doing. Fighting back a smile, Murdoch refocused on his task.

Could it be that I've found something this apparently ageless guy hasn't done before?

He barely suppressed a chuckle at his thoughts.

That slight slip of attention cost him.

Murdoch hadn't noticed that when the tree had snapped the fence post, it'd broken the nail holding that strand to it as well. When he snapped it, the side not trapped under the tree went flying. On instinct, Murdoch ducked.

The strand went zinging to his left.

A startled cry followed by a gasp caused Murdoch to jerk his attention in that direction.

Shock flooded him upon seeing Malakai standing there — Malakai with a streak of blood pooling up from the underside of his forearm, which he had lifted to protect his head.

Even as Murdoch registered the surprise and pain etched across Malakai's handsome features, the exquisite scent of the guy's blood blanketed his mind with an uncontrollable need to taste.

Murdoch was at Malakai's side in an instant, gripping his wrist. Taking in the beads of fluid, he inhaled the heady fragrance of iron and . . . something else . . . something . . .

Unable to help his need to figure out what that something was, Murdoch lifted Malakai's arm toward his mouth. He felt a hint of resistance from the other paranormal, but a tightening of his muscles pulled the guy through it. Plus, the way Malakai's expression turned heavy-lidded told Murdoch that he wasn't the only one feeling that same . . . something.

Sticking out his tongue, Murdoch slowly swiped up Malakai's flesh from just above his elbow all the way up to the palm of his hand. He groaned at the delicious, lightly spicy, iron-rich flavor. His eyes nearly rolled to the back of his head, and his knees grew weak, barely keeping him on his feet.

Unable to resist, Murdoch did it a second time, then a third.

Except, by then, either due to his vampiric saliva's healing abilities or Malakai's own speedy healing, there was no more blood to be had.

Groaning, Murdoch felt his fangs ache in a way he'd never before experienced. His cock throbbed insistently behind his fly, and he barely managed to press the heel of his palm against the base of his dick to stem his sudden urge to orgasm. The desire to sink his fangs deep, deep into Malakai's arm so he could drink his fill nearly took him to his knees. He barely managed to resist the impulse, but he did it, raising his head to stare in shock at the other male.

Seeing the way Malakai's lips were parted and the way he panted harshly with each breath caused a sense of smug satisfaction within Murdoch. How the guy's eyes were heavy-lidded and his cheeks were flushed were all indicators of arousal.

Arousal.

Murdoch's senses sang as the implications slammed through him. *Wait. What the hell?* Jerking back, he released Malakai's arm and took a step backward. On the rocky terrain, he nearly lost his balance.

When Malakai reached toward him, Murdoch lifted his hand to ward him away. The other man paused, a concerned light filling his aqua eyes.

Blowing out a harsh breath, Murdoch managed to find his voice. "You're my beloved." Pain filled him as he watched Malakai grimace. "You knew, and you didn't tell me. You hid it." Shaking his head, Murdoch rubbed his chest as if he could massage away an internal discomfort that he didn't think he could ever reach. "You don't want me, do you?"

Malakai's eyes widened. A stricken look took over him. He shook his head once, his gaze never wavering.

"I want you, my *stella guida*," Malakai claimed. "Never doubt that."

"Then why hide from me?" Murdoch demanded even as

he tried to place that particular endearment. He knew he'd heard it before.

With a pained expression, Malakai admitted, "I met you while you were professing your love for another. I didn't know what to do."

Okay. That made sense . . . sort of. Except, beloveds were sacrosanct in the paranormal world. They trumped all.

Was there a different reason Malakai hid their connection? Murdoch knew he had to be missing something.

If only I knew what the hell he was!

CHAPTER SIX

Knowing that explanation wasn't everything, Malakai tried to find the words for the rest of what he'd been considering. The feel of his tongue sliding over his skin had created sensations he'd never dreamed of. He wanted more of them, but he wasn't certain how to go about getting them.

It had hurt when Murdoch had moved away from his touch. He wanted to pull his vampire into his arms and soothe away the uncertainty he scented on him.

Making a decision, Malakai growled, "You are my *stella guida*." He stalked forward. "My guiding star. My reason for being." Grabbing Murdoch's upper arms, Malakai tugged his vampire flush to his chest. He wrapped one arm tightly around Murdoch's waist, reveling in the feel of the male pressed against his own body. "And I am your beloved." Lifting his palm to cradle Murdoch's jaw, he explained, "But you must still choose me. I didn't want you to be forced to do that simply because of vampire biology." After a glance around the remote area, Malakai refocused on Murdoch, peering into his stunning blue eyes. "That's why I followed you out here. So we could have time to get to know each other. So I could find out if there was a chance you'd choose me over someone from your past." Grimacing, he added, "Perhaps that was selfish of me, me knowing and keeping you in the dark, but the idea of being rejected, I—"

Malakai paused, uncertain how to finish that without sounding like a fool.

"You were afraid," Murdoch supplied, his voice gentle. His

eyes softened, and an understanding smile curved his lips. "Now that, I can understand." To Malakai's pleasure, Murdoch brought his hands up and rested his palms on his pectorals, rubbing lightly. "Just because the fates have deemed us beloveds doesn't mean it'll be a walk in the park." Twisting his lips into a wry smile, Murdoch added, "Although, I'm really glad you're another paranormal because it makes it easier, in my opinion. We already understand our urges." He slid his palms higher until he cradled Malakai's neck, causing the hairs at his nape to stand on end. "And for the record, Malakai, I would always choose you. You're my beloved."

A loud crack like the boom of thunder sounded through the air. Magickal energy rushed through the area on the wind, causing goose bumps to rise on Malakai's flesh. His hairs stood on end as a rush of awareness flooded his body—the start of their bond.

Murdoch's eyes widened, and he glanced up at the sky. Confusion clouded his blue eyes just as quickly as he returned his attention to Malakai. Then his jaw sagged open.

"Holy fuck," Murdoch whispered, realization dawning on his features. "You're an angel."

Clearing his throat, Malakai nodded once. "I am."

"I just started our bond."

"You did," Malakai confirmed.

Then, after a second of hesitation, Malakai dropped not only his glamour, but his scent suppression as well. With bated breath, he waited for his *stella guida*'s response. He watched as Murdoch's lips parted, his attention slipping over his shoulder.

Malakai knew what had Murdoch's focus—his wings.

"They're beautiful," Murdoch murmured in clear awe. Lifting one hand from Malakai's neck, he began reaching for them, then hesitated. Meeting Malakai's eyes once more, Murdoch asked, "Am I allowed to touch?"

Smiling, Malakai told him, "You may touch me anytime, anywhere."

The smile that broke out over Murdoch's features sent Malakai's pulse soaring. His breath caught in his throat, and a flush of heat coursed through his body. When the vampire once again reached over his shoulder and slid his fingertips along the feathers of one wing, Malakai didn't know which was better — the gentle touch of his *stella guida* or the obvious pleasure radiating from Murdoch.

I'll go with pleasing my vampire.

After a moment of light petting, Murdoch drew back. He peered into Malakai's eyes and grinned at him. "You know, one of the reasons I decided to allow you to stay with me was because I was worried you were a danger to my coven." With a wink, he continued, "Guess that's not a concern, huh?"

Malakai returned Murdoch's grin. "Not a danger. No." Rubbing his hands up and down his vampire's back, he added, "Quite the opposite, actually. I'll protect our home with everything in me." Unable to help himself, Malakai smirked. "Which is a considerable amount of power, truth be told."

Murdoch tipped his head to the side a little. "You're willing to stay here? With me?"

Shrugging, Malakai told him, "We can go anywhere you want, make anywhere home. It's up to you." Then he sobered. "Except my realm. Now that I've found you, I won't be going there much because you can't live there."

"I can't?" Murdoch looked a little offended, his next words confirming his annoyance. "What? Your people have a problem with other paranormals?"

Malakai quickly shook his head. "No, not at all." While he knew there were some angels who thought those of other planes were beneath them, they were few and far between. "The realm itself isn't safe for you. It's too . . . *much*."

"Much?" Murdoch frowned. "How do you mean?"

41

Searching for a proper explanation, Malakai slowly told him, "The air is clearer. The sun brighter. The grass greener. Colors are more vibrant, and there's a peaceful air to the place that makes anyone who isn't an angel just want to sit down, relax, and take it all in."

"Sounds like paradise," Murdoch stated, telling Malakai that he hadn't explained it quite right.

"It is," Malakai confirmed. "Except, any creature except an angel finds it *too* perfect. Eventually, you'd become so sluggish that you'd just lie down and die."

Murdoch's eyes widened. "Wow. Okay." Shaking his head, he gave him a wry smile. "So, really short visits only. Got it."

Malakai smiled back, appreciating that Murdoch understood. "So—" The scuff of hooves on rock as one of their horses shifted their weight drew his attention back to their surroundings. "So, I guess we should get back to work."

"Sure." Murdoch peered around before returning his attention to Malakai. Petting Malakai's jaw, he stated, "After you kiss me."

Drifting his focus to Murdoch's lips, Malakai admitted, "Just as I've never been attracted to anyone, I've never kissed anyone, either. I hope I'm not bad at it."

Murdoch's blue eyes filled with warmth. "Not possible." Sliding his hand around to cradle the back of Malakai's neck, he exerted a bit of pressure as he assured, "I'll guide you."

Malakai nodded. Then he tightened his arms around Murdoch's back as he followed his vampire's guiding hands. He dipped his head down. Seeing how Murdoch tipped his head one way just a little and feeling the pressure of his vampire's hand, Malakai tilted his head in the opposite direction, just as he'd seen other couples do.

Then, for the first time in his life, Malakai felt the press of lips against his own. He found the contact softer than he would have imagined. As Murdoch rubbed his dry lips against Malakai's own, he felt the vampire increase the pressure.

Then Murdoch nipped Malakai's bottom lip, drawing a surprised gasp from him. That must have been what he wanted, for in the next instant, his *stella guida* eased his tongue into his mouth. Malakai accepted it, touching it with his own.

Deep masculine flavors burst across his taste buds, lighting them up. Moaning softly, wanting more, he lapped against Murdoch's tongue again. It wasn't enough.

Malakai slid his hand up and threaded it into Murdoch's hair, knocking his hat from his head. Using the hold, he tipped his vampire's head back a smidge. Then he pushed his tongue into Murdoch's mouth, the move allowing him to taste his *stella guida* fully.

Delicious. Better than ambrosia.

Reveling in the exquisite, masculine taste, Malakai lapped over his tongue and mapped his mouth. He licked over his teeth. When Malakai reached Murdoch's fangs, he explored those pointed appendages, wondering what they would feel like embedded in his neck.

Upon hearing Murdoch's moan, Malakai groaned with satisfaction. His dick throbbed behind his fly, and his hips bucked instinctually, pushing it into Murdoch's hard stomach. Feeling an answering hardness pressing into his thigh, he groaned again.

Sliding one hand to Murdoch's muscled butt-cheek, Malakai used the hold to shift his *stella guida*. He spread his legs wider, lowering his stance. Soon, he felt his vampire's hard flesh pressed against his own.

Even through several layers of fabric, the pressure felt better than anything Malakai could have possibly imagined.

When Murdoch tore his mouth away from him, Malakai feared he'd done something wrong. The heady moan that escaped the man coupled with the shudder of his body rectified that misconception. His words helped, too.

"F-Fuck, Mal," Murdoch rasped. He pressed his forehead against Malakai's chest as another tremble worked through him. "Gonna c-come."

"Yessss," Malakai rumbled, continuing to rock them together. His balls felt heavy, aching in a way he'd never felt before. The instinctual need for relief drove him. "Want you to. Want to give you pleasure."

Murdoch growled as his body seized against Malakai. For a second, he worried, having no experience with pleasures of the flesh. Had he done something wrong?

Then the delicious aroma of Murdoch's salty seed flooded the air.

Malakai inhaled deeply, reveling in that smell. The knowledge that he'd driven his *stella guida* to such heights sent his own pleasure soaring. His testicles pulled tight, and he found his body pitching over that same precipice.

Moaning and shuddering, Malakai reeled as his senses experienced the delight of orgasm for the first time in his existence. He mentally flew as he clung to Murdoch. He feared that if he released his vampire, he might float away.

After Malakai wasn't certain how long, he felt Murdoch's hands stroking down his back. He hummed appreciatively at the soothing touches. His chest still heaved as he struggled to catch his breath.

"Wow," Malakai mumbled, finally finding his breath. "That was . . . I don't know what that was."

"Yeah." Murdoch slowly lifted his head, offering him a crooked smile. His cheeks were flushed, and his blue eyes gleamed. "If standing here kissing and rutting causes an orgasm like that, I can't imagine how epic actual sex with you will be."

Malakai grinned, satisfaction filling him. "I look forward to finding out with you."

"Me, too," Murdoch replied as he seemed to be having just as much trouble catching his breath. Then he looked down toward their crotches and grimaced. "Although, the resulting mess will make work a little uncomfortable if we don't change."

About that time, Malakai registered what Murdoch was talking about. His seed had originally been hot and smooth, but drying against his fly, it was quickly becoming cold and tacky. Humming, Malakai eased his hold on Murdoch.

"Since I helped make this mess," Malakai told him with a smile. "I should clean it up."

Murdoch waggled his brows as a smirk curved his lips. "What did you have in mind?"

Malakai knew he was missing something even as he waved his hand between their flies and murmured a cleaning spell. Normally he used it to sanitize his sword, but he knew it would work for their clothes and skin just as well. Seconds later, they were clean.

"Oh." Murdoch stared up at him, surprise in his eyes. "That's nifty."

"Thank you."

Murdoch leaned down and picked up his hat. "Well, I guess we should get back to work." With a wink as he settled it on his head, Murdoch added, "I can't wait to make camp this evening so we can get to know each other even better."

The growl in Murdoch's tone caused even one as inexperienced as Malakai to catch on to his innuendo.

His breath catching in his throat, Malakai murmured, "I look forward to it."

CHAPTER SEVEN

Murdoch's body still continued to ping pleasantly from his epic orgasm, even after fixing the fence. He'd plotted the location along with notes needed to complete a better fix. Plus, the large downed limb could be cut up for firewood.

Back on horseback, Murdoch led the way along the fence line at a ground-eating jog. He glanced over his shoulder every few minutes and always spotted Malakai a couple of paces behind him. The man — *angel, holy shit, my beloved is an angel* — sported a relaxed expression as he took in the scenery.

His mind still reeled with everything that had just happened. He would need to call Master Jaymes that evening to let him know of his status change. Not only did he need to pack up his stuff to vacate the quarters he'd shared with Nester, but he needed to ask for quarters to be built a little ways back on the property.

Murdoch couldn't expect his angel beloved to hide his nature all the time. Plus, he loved looking at Malakai's stunning wings. The feathers adorning the large appendages were a gorgeous mix of tans and browns.

They'd felt amazing, too.

Malakai had explained how his glamour spell hid his aura as well as his wings. They were still there, however. The angel had to be careful about who was behind him at any given time, since in general, he didn't care for others touching his wings.

Murdoch felt blessed that he would have the privilege to pet them any time he wished.

"Will your coven really build us our own secluded home?"

Upon hearing Malakai's question, Murdoch eyed him curiously. "They will, but how did you come to that idea?"

Malakai grimaced as he tapped his temple. "Sorry. One of an angel's gifts is reading the minds of others." He quickly hurried to add, "Assuming they're thinking about something with enough emotional intent."

"Huh." Murdoch frowned. "As a vampire, I always knew I'd develop a mind-link with my beloved, but to have you able to read random shit?" After a second, he admitted, "I'm not certain how I feel about it. Isn't it . . . intrusive?"

To Murdoch's relief, Malakai chuckled, obviously not offended. The fact that his beloved had removed the suppression spell so he could scent him helped, too. His vampire nature needed to be reassured that he was pleasing the other half of his soul.

"I don't mean to laugh at you," Malakai began, a twinkle in his aqua eyes. "But as a vampire, you read minds and manipulate them on a regular basis to get a donor. How is my catching thoughts and using them to spread peace, harmony, love, and joy in the world any different?"

"Huh. Said like that." Murdoch scoffed, shaking his head. "Nope. Not different much at all."

"If you wish, I'll teach you how to block your thoughts from me." Malakai smiled warmly at him. "As my *stella guida*, once we've finished our bond, you'll have that gift."

"Oh, very nice. Thanks." Then something else occurred to Murdoch. "Uh, probably don't try to read the thoughts of bonded couples because they're normally pretty racy."

Malakai nodded his understanding. "Wise words, my star."

A fence broken away from a post appeared ahead, drawing Murdoch's attention. He stopped next to it, realizing it was a broken nail. After a quick fix of replacing it, he swung back into the saddle, and they moved on.

As Murdoch unsaddled his horse, he realized he'd had the best day of fence-checking he'd ever experienced. Malakai's presence relaxed him, and they had shared many past experiences. Murdoch had been quite shocked to learn that his beloved truly didn't know how old he was. Malakai had simply been made by his creator at the dawn of man—human and paranormal alike—and as an angel, it was his job to help balance humanity emotionally and spiritually.

"That's a big job," Murdoch had commented. "And getting harder every year with how many humans are populating the earth."

Malakai had sighed deeply and nodded. "It is indeed." Then he'd gotten a vacant look on his face as he obviously thought more on that.

Murdoch had dropped the subject and kept them moving.

"Can I help set up camp?" Malakai asked. Shamrock was already munching on the grass under her hooves, having been tied to the high-line Murdoch had set up for the animals.

"I didn't bring a tent," Murdoch admitted as he tied Duke a ways down from Shamrock. Heading to Hazel, he added, "I have staples of rice and beans, dried meats, packets of pork and beans, stuff like that." Murdoch didn't eat fancy while out riding fence. "They taste best heated over a fire. Do you wanna gather firewood while I take care of Hazel?"

"I'd be happy to." Malakai started to turn away, but he paused and turned back to him.

To Murdoch's pleasure, his beloved cupped his jaw and pecked a quick kiss to his lips. Then, with a smile, he headed away from him. His own grin firmly in place, Murdoch made quick work of removing Hazel's gear and rubbing her down. Out of the corner of his eye, he watched Malakai scour the area for wood, piling it off to the side. He even gathered a number of rocks to make a fire pit.

While tying Hazel to the high-line, Murdoch realized Malakai could probably have done it all by magick. "Why didn't you just wave your hand and do it automatically," he asked curiously. "Not that it wasn't sexy as hell to watch you bend over in those jeans."

After letting out a deep chuckle, Malakai explained, "As a rule, we don't use magick out in the open." He lifted his hand, palm up, and swung it in an arc around them. "While we are quite a ways out, we are in a fairly open area. There's no telling who might stumble upon us."

Even as Murdoch nodded, understanding what Malakai was telling him, he pointed at his beloved. "But your wings are showing."

Malakai smiled as he shook his head. Reaching out, he slid his arm around Murdoch's waist and pulled him close. Murdoch was only too willing to go to his lover and rested his palms on his expansive chest.

"I amended my glamour spell," Malakai told him. "The only one who will always see me as I am, is you."

"Wow," Murdoch breathed. "Really?"

Nodding, Malakai shared, "I never want to hide anything from you."

Malakai dipped his head and pecked a kiss to Murdoch's lips. Evidently, he was really taking to kissing, which Murdoch appreciated. Wrapping his own arms around his beloved, Murdoch returned his embrace.

"I really like that," Murdoch admitted. "No secrets."

"Not from each other," Malakai confirmed. "I'll of course tell your master what I am. Show him. He'll need to know."

Murdoch nodded. "Makes sense. Maybe at our next coven barbeque, you can briefly show everyone. They'll need to understand so they can protect your identity."

Malakai hummed. "Makes sense."

A second later, Malakai sealed his mouth over Murdoch's own. He pushed his tongue between his lips and explored him deeply. Malakai didn't ease up until Murdoch gasped for breath and his cock throbbed behind his fly.

With a soft groan, Malakai began moving back in for another kiss when Murdoch's stomach grumbled.

Chuckling, Malakai shook his head. "Time to feed you, my vampire."

Even as Murdoch knew that Malakai referred to food, his attention riveted on the pulse of his beloved's neck. His mouth began to water for a whole new reason. The small sampling of his angel's blood had barely whetted his appetite, and his hunger for a true taste had been increasing all day.

It didn't help that Murdoch hadn't fed on fresh blood in almost a week, and that had been from Nester.

"I'll feed that need this evening, too," Malakai assured, telling Murdoch that he'd picked up on his thoughts. "I'll always care for you."

After another quick peck, Malakai eased away from Murdoch. "I'll start the fire if you want to grab the food. You mentioned you didn't have a tent," he continued, moving toward his woodpile. "I can magick one up if you'd like."

"Really?" Murdoch headed to gather food and cooking utensils. "Can you create anything?"

"Technically, I'm not actually creating anything," Malakai told him as he set up the wood in the fire. "I use a transmutation spell. It turns something existing into something else." Pointing at a nearby rock, he continued, "For example."

Then Malakai whispered a few words in a language Murdoch didn't recognize. An instant later, the rock was gone. In its place rested an equally gray, fluffy bedroll.

"That's how I made the gloves. I turned part of a bush into a replica of your gloves, fitted to me."

"Wow." Murdoch couldn't think of anything else to say.

Malakai didn't seem to need it. He just grinned at him, then returned his attention to building a fire. As Murdoch carried a pot, silverware, and the saddlebags given to him by Vaughn toward the fire, he saw Malakai hold his palm toward the cone of wood.

A second later, a small flame burst to life within the teepee. It grew swiftly, and Murdoch felt the prickle that he was beginning to recognize as Malakai using magick.

"Okay, that certainly makes it easy." Murdoch grinned as he placed the pot on one of the rocks making up the fire ring.

Malakai winked at him. "And if anyone is around to see, they'll probably just think I have excellent fire-making skills."

Murdoch barked a laugh as he began pulling items out of the saddlebag. "Oh, nice. Vaughn sent dried fruits, nuts, and seeds to munch on." He quickly opened the bag of dried apples and popped a slice into his mouth. Humming appreciatively around his mouthful, Murdoch held it out to Malakai.

"Thank you," his angel said as he took a slice.

Chewing, Murdoch continued to search through the contents. Everything in the bag was homemade by Vaughn and in vacuum-sealed pouches. Spotting a pair that were both labeled pot roast, Murdoch pulled them out.

As Murdoch looked at the food in the clear package, his taste buds salivating at what he knew would be delicious beef and perfectly flavored broth and vegetables, a thought occurred to him.

Lifting his focus to Malakai, Murdoch asked, "Are angels vegetarians?"

"No," Malakai instantly replied. Arching his brow, he eyed him curiously. "What made you think of that?"

Murdoch shrugged. "I'm not sure. You're from a different plane, right?" After seeing Malakai's nod, he admitted, "I thought maybe there could be dietary restrictions that you had to follow."

Malakai shook his head, smiling at him. "No. Just with any society, what we decide to eat is purely a personal choice." With a grin, he added, "And I can tell you, I absolutely love your chef's sausage, egg, and cheese breakfast burritos. Amazing."

Laughing, Murdoch nodded. "I completely agree. Add a bit of picante sauce, and they're even more epic."

"Yes!"

With a grin, Murdoch grew a talon—a sharp, three-inch nail that extended from a vampire's fingers to use during a fight—and sliced open the first package of pot roast. After pouring it into his pot, he did the same with the second. He tossed the used packages into the fire to burn, thereby eliminating garbage with food on it, which could draw in predators.

After placing the metal cover on the pot, Murdoch retrieved his tarp and bedroll. He spread them on the ground, creating a place for them to sit and relax while they waited.

CHAPTER EIGHT

Watching Murdoch toss another log onto the fire, Malakai relaxed on his vampire's spread bedroll, which his *stella guida* had placed on the tarp. According to Murdoch, that would diminish the amount of cold that soaked up from the ground. They would use the bedroll Malakai had created to spread over them.

Malakai listened to the fire crackle merrily, and he relaxed on the blanket. Alternating between staring at the stars and watching Murdoch move around camp, he admired his vampire. His *stella guida* moved confidently, putting away the cookware.

When Malakai had offered to clean everything with magick, Murdoch had smirked and quirked one brow. "Is that because you're in a hurry to lie down with me?"

Even hearing the teasing tone in Murdoch's voice, Malakai had still felt his blood heat and his body quicken with anticipation. He would be able to hold his vampire all night long. He could hardly wait.

"Yes," Malakai had declared. "I want you in my arms as swiftly as possible."

"Then clean away," Murdoch had encouraged.

Malakai had done it, and now, in just another moment, Murdoch would be joining him on the blanket. Staring at the stars gleaming overhead, he took several slow deep breaths. His body burned with anticipation, making it difficult to relax.

"Everything okay?"

Malakai snapped his attention to Murdoch, who stood sil-
houetted against the fire, his face in shadows.

A need to touch filling him, Malakai lifted one hand. "Will
you join me?"

"I'd love to," Murdoch told him, kicking off his boots. He
then pointed at Malakai's footwear. "Can I help you remove
those?"

Malakai shook his head. "No need." Then he kicked them
off. "I'm not certain what the protocol is here," he added as
he watched Murdoch toss his hat onto the nearby saddlebag.
"Should we undress each other or . . . begin clothed?"

"I plan to remove your shirt shortly," Murdoch told him,
slipping out of his coat. After rolling it into a bundle, he lowered to his knees and held it out. "Our pillow."

Murdoch took the offered item and tucked it behind his
head.

"Question," Murdoch began, unbuttoning his flannel shirt.
"How do you deal with shirts and your wings?"

Chuckling, Malakai admitted, "I manifest my clothing di-
rectly onto my body. That way, I don't have to worry about
it."

Smirking, Murdoch pinned a look on him that could only
have been called hungry. "Does that mean I can shred that off
you?" He lifted his hand and grew his talons. "You can make
a new one, right?"

Malakai sucked in a quick breath, a wash of heat slamming
through him. He didn't know why he found the idea of his
stella guida tearing his clothes from him to be sexually excit-
ing, but he did, his body flooding with need. Goose bumps
broke out over his body, and he couldn't help the way his
wings twitched . . . as did his erection.

Murdoch's blue eyes narrowed and began bleeding to red.
"Oh, my beloved," he crooned, his nostrils flaring. "You do
like that idea, don't you?"

With a quick move, Murdoch yanked his flannel and undershirt from his body and tossed them aside. He began to lean forward before hesitating. His palm slid over Malakai's feathered wing where it rested on the blanket to either side of him.

"Can I lean on your wings?" Murdoch asked, his brows furrowing. "I don't want to hurt you."

"You can," Malakai assured, pleased by Murdoch's show of concern. "They're quite resilient and can easily take your weight."

Murdoch grunted, a sound of pleasure. "Good."

Then Murdoch rested his weight on his left hand. He slid the sharp talons on his right hand beneath the fabric at Malakai's collar. The feel and sight of the razor-like appendages sliding across the sensitive skin of his neck should have worried Malakai, but all he felt was anticipation.

Malakai's stomach fluttered. His nipples beaded. Even his erection twitched behind his fly, and he felt the unmistakable sensation of fluid leaking from him.

Oh. Oh, wow!

Murdoch sliced his talons downward, tearing the fabric in one long, smooth glide. Feeling the ever-so-slight scrape of his vampire's dangerous appendages skimming over his flesh, he felt the hairs on his arms stand on end. Heat erupted within his veins, shooting tendrils of need throughout him.

"Oh, my handsome beloved," Murdoch rumbled, his voice deepening. "My angel." He separated the ruined flaps, revealing Malakai's chest before he slid his palms back up his flesh. "So very sexy."

As Murdoch continued to cut off Malakai's polo shirt, the blue of his eyes quickly bled to red. When Murdoch had completely destroyed his shirt, leaving his torso bare, he met Malakai's gaze. His *stella guida's* desire easily burned within the depths of his gaze.

"All mine." Murdoch's voice took on a reverent tone. "My

angel. All mine."

Then Murdoch lowered toward Malakai. Instead of capturing his lips, his vampire brushed a soft kiss to the groove of his hip just above his jeans. He then began mouthing more kisses over his stomach, tracing the delineated lines of his abdominals with his teeth and tongue. At the same time, Murdoch traced every inch of his skin with his fingertips, sensitizing every bit of him.

Before not long at all, Malakai shivered and trembled, and it had nothing to do with the cooling evening air. Instead, he felt hot, so very hot. His blood fired through his veins, and he struggled to control each breath.

"You're mine, aren't you, Malakai?" Murdoch rumbled, peering up his torso with a feral expression tightening his features. "Mine to love, to care for, to pleasure and share my life with. Only mine."

"Yours," Malakai replied breathlessly, holding Murdoch's gaze squarely. He saw not only his desire, but also his sheer need for that to be true. Knowing from where it stemmed — the betrayal of his ex — Malakai continued, "I am yours and only yours, Murdoch. I have never touched another, and I never will. You're it for me, my *stella guida*. You're my star."

Groaning, Murdoch levered up and captured Malakai's mouth in a bruising kiss. He plundered him, his kiss desperate. Malakai wrapped his arms around Murdoch and let his vampire have his way. He would always give him whatever he needed.

After a few minutes, Murdoch gentled the kiss. He slowly eased it to an end before parting their mouths. Lifting his head, he peered deep into Murdoch's troubled gaze.

"I didn't used to be so broken," Murdoch whispered, his brows furrowing. "I — " He paused and shook his head. "I-I'm not certain how gentle I can be. I" — then Murdoch frowned — "don't have any lube."

Malakai smiled his understanding. "You don't need to be gentle with me," he assured, rubbing his hands up and down Murdoch's back, enjoying the opportunity to do a little exploring of his own. He loved the feel of Murdoch's bare flesh beneath his palms. "I'm a paranormal," he reminded him upon seeing his troubled look. "And I can create lube, remember?"

Putting word to deed, Malakai pulled his hand away from Murdoch. He cupped his hand and murmured a few words. A column of dirt rose from the ground nearby and swirled through the air, spiraling in a mini-tornado to land on his palm. As the dirt settled, it transformed into a translucent fluid.

Groaning, Murdoch stared at the slick for a few seconds before focusing on Malakai again. "I'm a switch," he whispered softly. "I can bottom for you for this first time."

Malakai could only guess at how difficult it had been for Murdoch to make that offer. His need perfumed the air in heady goodness. His *stella guida's* body practically vibrated with it.

"I am yours," Malakai reminded him. "And I want to feel you sink deep into my body, connecting us together in the most primal of ways."

Groaning, Murdoch nodded. He pushed away, reaching for the button of his jeans. "I need you so very badly," he mumbled, shoving his pants down his thighs. Then he reached for Malakai's fly and quickly undid his, too. "I promise I'll woo you properly another time. I"—he blew out a harsh breath and paused to meet Malakai's gaze—"never realized I could need someone so much."

Planting his feet, Malakai lifted his hips in invitation. "Then take what is yours, Murdoch. I want you, too." He narrowed his eyes and whispered, "Should I prepare myself for you?"

While Malakai had never done that before, he understood the concept. Plus, he could do it with magick. It would be such a simple manipulation of a leather stretching spell—something he'd had to do many times over the years to create a sword scabbard when one grew too old.

To Malakai's surprise, Murdoch whined as he reached down and gripped the base of his erection. His dick appeared dark red and thick. A bead of pre-cum glistened at the tip, and Malakai felt a surprising desire to lick it off of him.

"Oh, gods, yessss," Murdoch hissed. His irises darkened to red once more, and his voice grew husky. He swiftly divested Malakai of his remaining clothing. "Yes, I want to see that."

Malakai figured Murdoch didn't realize how he intended to do it, but that was okay. He would figure it out swiftly enough. Rolling onto his knees and his clean hand, he reached backward with the one still cupping the lube.

While spreading his legs and putting his ass in the air felt extremely odd, Malakai banished the sensation. Hearing Murdoch's throaty groan and feeling his hands rubbing over his hips helped. By feel, Malakai easily found his opening and pushed in one forefinger.

Whispering the necessary spell, Malakai sent the fluid coating his hand oozing into his chute. His muscled stretched and relaxed. The odd sensation created an oddly empty feeling within him, and his erection bobbed between his legs.

Turning his head, Malakai took in Murdoch's red-eyed gaze. His vampire's attention was pinned to his ass. His lips were slightly parted, and sweat gleamed on his flesh, glittering in the firelight.

"Now," Malakai insisted. Reaching back, he gripped Murdoch's gorgeous length, spreading the remaining lube on him, drawing his forever love's attention. "I need you, my *stella guida*. Claim me."

Murdoch's nostrils flared, and the erection in Malakai's

grip flexed.

"Mine," Murdoch hissed, his fangs gleaming in the light of the fire. "All mine."

"Yours," Malakai confirmed.

When Murdoch moved closer behind him, Malakai released his vampire's prick. He arched his back, presenting for his star as best as he knew how. Feeling Murdoch's cap press to his hole, Malakai breathed out a long breath.

Just that easily, Murdoch's erection slid in and in . . . and in.

Malakai's chute muscles stretched, allowing Murdoch to bury his length within his body in one long, smooth glide. While he felt the stretch, there was no pain. Upon feeling Murdoch's groin pressed tight against his butt cheeks, Malakai knew he'd taken all his vampire had to give.

Humming with pleasure at his accomplishment, Malakai clenched and released experimentally. His vampire groaned, so he did it once more.

Murdoch draped over him, wrapping one arm around his torso while using the other to take some of his weight. "Oh, my beloved," he groaned into his ear. "Gods, so good."

The need for something . . . for more . . . tightened Malakai's gut. He trembled in Murdoch's hold, a shiver working down his spine when he felt his vampire's teeth scraping across his tendon.

"Please, Mur," Malakai rumbled, panting. "I . . . I *need*."

"I know what you need," Murdoch claimed.

Then Murdoch proved exactly that. He eased his prick most of the way out of Malakai, adjusted his angle, and thrust back into him. Sparks danced across Malakai's vision, and a spike of heat flooded his groin.

"Oh, Mur!" Malakai cried, and Murdoch did it again.

Even as Malakai recognized that Murdoch was pegging his prostate over and over, he struggled to process the mind-bending sensations flooding him. His body burned in a way that caused his balls to tingle. He couldn't stop the way his body arched and pushed back into each of Murdoch's ruts, chasing more of the heady feelings his lover created.

"Come for me, Malakai," Murdoch demanded gruffly. "Show me how much you love my claiming."

As if wired to obey, Malakai did exactly that. His eyes nearly rolled to the back of his head as his orgasm crashed over him. He soared on the blissful ecstasy as his erection unloaded onto the blanket beneath him.

Hearing Murdoch's roar, feeling him bury himself as deeply as possible, followed by the heat of his vampire's release, Malakai groaned for a whole new reason. His bond strengthened, heating his blood anew.

Then Murdoch's teeth pierced his neck. The sucking on his flesh shot straight to his balls.

Malakai tipped his head back and roared as a second orgasm blind-sided him.

Panting harshly, Malakai slowly came back to himself. He registered two things. First, Murdoch still remained draped over him. Second, Malakai's erection continued to ache.

Knowing exactly what he needed, Malakai eased forward. The move jostled his *stella guida*, and Murdoch groaned while easing away and out of him.

As soon as Murdoch was clear, Malakai twisted and pounced. He tackled his vampire to the blanket. Grinning down at the surprised male, he claimed, "Now, it's my turn."

With a grin and a feral growl, his eyes red once more, Murdoch wrapped his legs around Malakai's waist in invitation.

"All yours," his vampire vowed.

"All mine."

Malakai set about proving that . . . several times throughout the night.

CHAPTER NINE

Deliciously sore—and not from riding in a saddle for almost three days straight—Murdoch led the way into the yard. As tired as he knew Duke was, the second the young gelding spotted the barn, he managed to perk up and increase his stride. His horse wasn't the only one of them eager to see home. Hazel brayed, receiving several whinnies in response.

Chuckling, Malakai murmured, "You'd think they'd been gone forever."

"They're just happy to be home." Murdoch grinned at Malakai. "I am, too."

Reaching across the distance, Malakai squeezed his upper arm. "So am I. I look forward to us starting our life together."

"Me, too," Murdoch agreed, anticipation warming his insides in a way that was in no way sexual. This was his beloved, and they were home. "We'll need to go see Master Jaymes first thing after untacking." He stopped Duke at the hitching post where he'd tacked up three days before. Malakai stopped beside him. Before swinging off his gelding, Murdoch reminded, "We'll need to know our new room assignment."

Too excited about discovering Malakai was his beloved, he had completely forgotten to contact Jaymes that first evening. He'd called him the following morning and informed him of two things. First, that Murdoch would need new quarters, since he could no longer stay with Nester. Second, he'd met his beloved in Malakai.

Master Jaymes had been extremely happy for him, his joy

filling his tone. When he'd learned that Malakai was an angel, he'd been a little shocked. Then he'd assured him that he would take care of Murdoch's belongings and had urged him to bring Malakai to his office upon their return.

They'd spent the rest of the trip riding fence, talking about their lives, and sharing their hopes for the future. To Murdoch's surprise, he'd learned that Malakai was a little disappointed that the surrogate hadn't worked out. He'd been interested in the idea of raising a young one, seeing as he'd never had a childhood of his own.

Murdoch had found it fascinating that angels were created fully formed. Of course, that didn't mean they hadn't gone through extensive training. He'd found Malakai's tales of his home realm intriguing.

Malakai had even promised to take him there, but as he'd explained, it would have to be an extremely short visit.

Safety first, and all that.

"Should I take Shamrock to the other stable?" Malakai asked, remaining in the saddle.

"We'll bed her down here," Murdoch told him. He had no desire to allow his newly bonded beloved out of his sight quite yet. "She deserves a few days of rest. Besides, she may turn into your personal mount unless you decide on another."

While most of the vampires didn't have a personal mount, a few did—like Second Gypsum and his big Friesian stallion, who happened to be Shamrock's sire. With Malakai being even bigger than his second—who stood a robust six-foot-five—there were only a couple of horses that would be able to handle his angel's size. He would have the option of choosing one of the others, but for now, Shamrock was it.

"I like Shamrock," Malakai claimed, rubbing the big mare's forehead. "She's a kind sweetheart."

"That she is," Murdoch agreed.

"Let's get these guys settled, then we can—"

"There you are. About time you got back."

Murdoch turned upon hearing Nester's angry shout.

Narrowing his eyes as he took in his ex-lover, he wondered what the hell he'd ever seen in the man. The hazel eyes he'd loved to peer into were narrowed and dark with anger. His full lips were curved into an angry scowl as he strode toward him, turning his boy-next-door features into something less-than-appealing. Even the tension in his body caused his usually sensual fluid movements to turn jerky.

"How dare you have your things moved out of our suite," Nester snarled, glaring. Lifting a hand, he pointed at him as he swiftly closed the distance. "You're mine, Murdoch, until I say otherwise. You can't—"

"That's not how a relationship works," Malakai cut in, stepping in front of Murdoch, stopping Nester from possibly poking him in the chest.

Murdoch stepped sideways just in time to see Nester jolt back a step.

Curling his lip, Nester swept his gaze up and down his lover. "I remember you," he declared. "You're the fucker who thought he owned the dining hall steps and got in my way." Nester crossed his arms over his chest and thrust out with his power. His eyes hazed red, and it was obvious that he was attempting to manipulate Malakai. "Move along, asshole, before I'm forced to move you."

Anger surged through Murdoch upon seeing another vampire—regardless of the fact that it was his cheater of an ex— trying to exert power over his beloved. Just as he took a step forward, he heard Malakai's deep rumbling chuckle.

"Oh, vampire," Malakai stated. "Your mind tricks have no hold on me." Shaking his head, he told him, "I know I had my scent suppressed before, but use your nose now." Leaning toward Nester, Malakai told him, "And it will tell you that I'm not human, nor should you try to mess with me."

Nester sucked in a sharp breath, which must have given

him enough of a whiff of Malakai for his scent to register. For an instant, the blood began to drain from his face. "What are you?" he hissed, narrowing his eyes at him. Just as quickly, his eyes widened, and he swung his gaze to Murdoch. "You fed from him? Took him as a donor?" Sneering, Nester shook his head. "And you yelled at me for taking donors without you. You're such a hypocrite." He tipped his chin up in a haughty fashion. "I forgive you. You can move your stuff back into our suite today."

"I'm not going to repeat myself." Murdoch crossed his arms over his chest. He couldn't believe he'd never seen this side of Nester—him acting like a selfish child. "While I understand that we never explicitly said we could *not* take outside donors, that was the kind of relationship I thought we had. For two years, I only slept with you and the people we shared." Doing his best to ignore the way Nester rolled his eyes, Murdoch told him, "But that was the kind of relationship I thought we had, and that's the kind of relationship I wanted out of someone who was not my beloved. It's over between us. Besides, I—"

"It's *not* over between us," Nester screamed. He even stamped his foot like a petulant child. "I'm not done with your ass. It's mine whenever I need a screw, and that's not changing until I say so. I—"

"Is there a problem here?"

Murdoch looked beyond Nester and spotted Abner Johnson. The big, burly redhead was their coven's human blacksmith. He was also mated with Pascal, one of the trio of dingo shifters who lived at the coven. Pascal's two brothers were bonded with vampires.

Nester curled his lip and sneered at Abner. "Nothing that concerns you, *human*." The way he said the word was more like a curse. "Be on your way with whatever." Nester flicked his fingers as if shoeing away a fly.

"Well, now," Abner replied, appearing unconcerned with Nester's ire. Instead, the blacksmith eyed Nester with a definite glint of contempt in his deep green eyes. "Considering you're holding up Murdoch and his friend from putting their horses away, you're holding me up, too." Looking down his nose at Nester—which was easy, considering the big human stood six-foot-four—and crossing his huge arms over his chest, Abner continued, "I think you should be on your way. I'm pretty sure Mathe is looking for you, considering I just finished having lunch with him and my mate's brother."

Mathe—a coven enforcer with the title of ranch foreman—was bonded with Pascal's younger brother, Julian. The eldest brother, Lucius, was bonded with the coven second, Gypsum.

Probably knowing better than to get into an altercation with someone—even a human—so close to the inner circle of the coven, Nester glowered as he began stalking away from them. Still, he hollered over his shoulder, "I expect to see you home in our suite after dinner, Murdoch."

"Don't hold your breath," Murdoch couldn't help but call back. Then he grinned and added, "Or maybe you should."

Tipping his head back, Abner laughed deeply.

A red-faced Nester cast an angry look over his shoulder. If looks could kill, Murdoch was damn certain they would all be dead, or maybe extremely maimed.

"Well, he's gonna cause you some problems, Murdoch," Abner stated, drawing closer. His mirth had faded, and he stared between them with a serious expression. "That vampire doesn't seem to realize his shit don't stink." Grimacing, Abner quickly added, "I know you were with him for a couple of years, and you're a nice guy, so, uh . . . maybe he has some redeeming qualities, but—"

Lifting his hands in placation, Murdoch quickly cut into the human's uncertain rambling. "No, I get it. He's being a douche, and I think he got used to certain privileges while be-ing coupled with me." He shook his head as he realized he'd sort of been taken advantage of. "I don't want to make excuses for him, but this change is probably out of the blue for him. I'm certain he'll get over it eventually."

Still appearing uncomfortable, Abner muttered, "If you say so." Then his attention shifted to Duke, Shamrock, and Hazel. "After such extensive work over rocky terrain, I want to check their shoes. I'll help you settle them in. I know you have some-where to be." A knowing smile curved Abner's lips as he eyed Malakai. He held out his hand. "I'm Abner Johnson. I'm sure I'll be seeing you around." After shaking, Abner headed to-ward Hazel. He walked backward a few steps as he waggled a finger between them. "And congrats, guys. Those around here who know are happy for you."

"Thanks, Abner," Murdoch replied with a grin. After grip-ping Malakai's fingers and giving them a light squeeze, he smiled at his lover and urged, "Let's get this done so we can get to our meeting."

Malakai nodded. "Sounds good."

Over thirty minutes later, walking hand in hand into the coven house with Malakai at his side, Murdoch couldn't have felt prouder. He spotted a number of smiles, surprised expres-sions, and even a jealous look or two. Unlike Nester, who was too busy making his demands known, those they passed in the common rooms immediately recognized the bond be-tween Murdoch and Malakai.

While Malakai received a number of questioning looks, telling Murdoch that they didn't recognize him for what he was, Boyd and Royce offered them both grins and big thumbs up.

Chuckling, Murdoch led the way upstairs. He turned into Master Jaymes's suite and stopped at the first door on the left.

After two knocks, he heard his master order for them to enter.

Doing as bidden, Murdoch opened the door. With his fingers twined with Malakai's, he entered his master's office for the second time in less than a week. He swept his gaze around the room, taking in the occupants, surprised to see nearly all of the inner circle.

Master Jaymes sat behind his desk with Paul on his lap. Gypsum and Lucius were in a similar position on a large, cushioned chair. Mathe sat on a small sofa with Julian and Pascal. Enforcers Rhyme and Clarice were there, too.

Evidently, Malakai picked up on something Murdoch didn't, for he tightened his hold on Murdoch's fingers and tugged him closer. As soon as he could, he slung his arm around Murdoch's waist and tucked him against his side.

"Master Jaymes?" Murdoch asked uncertainly. "Is something wrong?"

Master Jaymes arched one brow and glanced around. Scoffing, he smirked as he urged Paul to his feet. Rising to stand next to him, he leaned forward and held out his hand.

"Good afternoon, Malakai. Welcome to the coven."

After Malakai shook hands with Master Jaymes, the head vampire waved a hand toward the remaining sofa. "Please, have a seat."

Obeying, Murdoch noticed Jaymes settling back on his chair. Paul immediately returned to his lap.

"Congratulations on your bonding, Murdoch. I'm truly happy for you," Master Jaymes told him, although his expression appeared serious. "Unfortunately, we do have a problem."

What else is new?

The corners of Malakai's lips twitched, telling Murdoch that he'd picked up on his thought.

CHAPTER TEN

Malakai barely refrained from laughing at Murdoch's mental snipe. With his arm slung across the back of the sofa, he teased his fingertips over his *stella guida's* opposite shoulder. He continued to keep his attention on Master Jaymes. To his surprise, Malakai wasn't picking up any thoughts from anyone in the room.

Huh. All these vampires seem to have excellent mental shields. Either that or the master knows how to shield those around him.

Those were the only explanation.

Malakai respected their power.

"What seems to be the problem, Master Jaymes," Murdoch asked, holding his master's gaze. "If it's about Nester, I'm aware he seems to be having a hard time letting go. We'll be careful of him until he accepts that it's over."

From the thoughts that had been drifting through Nester's mind, Malakai wouldn't hold his breath on how long that would take.

"Actually, no." Master Jaymes furrowed his brows. "Although after he took a swing at Mathe when he and Boyd went to collect your things, he's already been warned to stay away from you." Growling softly, the master grumbled, "We'll definitely be speaking to him about that."

"I'm confused, then, Master." Murdoch sounded and scented of it, too. "What problem can I help with?"

Opening a folder on his desk, Master Jaymes peered at the paper on top. "I received a petition from a Lorain Caldsyn."

He focused on Murdoch. "She says you're in breach of contract with her."

Murdoch frowned. "Really?" He glanced at Malakai, his confusion apparent. "That's weird."

"So you do know her?" Second Gypsum pressed.

Murdoch immediately nodded. "Yes. Lorain was supposed to act as a surrogate for me and Nester. She was supposed to be artificially inseminated, although we hadn't decided whose sperm to use, yet." His cheeks darkened in an obvious blush, but his voice remained steady as he revealed, "I walked in on Nester fucking Lorain. I walked out and told Doctor Sutherland that their services would no longer be required."

"Ah." Master Jaymes's brows furrowed, and his jaw tightened. "She's still demanding you either go through with it or that you pay the back-out clause fee."

"Seriously?" Murdoch growled, anger flooding his scent. "How can she demand that when she was fucking around? She could be pregnant."

Malakai tightened his hold around Murdoch's waist, holding him in place. "May we speak with Lorain?" As an angel, he should easily be able to read the true intentions of a human.

Shaking his head, Jaymes revealed, "She refuses to be alone with any vampire again." He frowned as he continued, "She also claims that Nester coerced her with his abilities, so she's not responsible for that."

"Is there probable cause to search Nester's mind?" Malakai asked, eyeing Master Jaymes. He figured as the coven master that he had the abilities to do it. "I'd offer my services, but I figure since I'm new here, that could cause problems."

Master Jaymes nodded, his smile turning rueful. "Unfortunately, yes. That would cause problems." Then his smile turned predatory. "But you are correct. I do need to confirm whether or not Nester coerced Lorain, since that will have a bearing on this situation." Turning his attention to Mathe, he ordered, "Locate Nester and bring him to my office in thirty minutes, please." Then he picked up the phone and eyed Murdoch. "Either way, you'll have to face Lorain. Are you willing to pay the fee in the back-out clause?"

"We'd rather have her fulfill the contract," Malakai stated, causing Murdoch to stiffen beside him. His *stella guida* stared at him with wide eyes. Smiling, Malakai skimmed the backs of his forefingers along his vampire's jaw as he stated, "I know how much you wanted to raise a child. I'd be happy to do that with you." Uncertainty filled him, and he quickly added, "Unless you don't want to raise one with me?"

Murdock continued to gape at him for several seconds before snapping his mouth shut. "I'd be honored to raise a child with you," he whispered. With wide eyes, Murdoch admitted, "It's just, we just met. We're still figuring out how to fit together. Do you really want to do that while caring for a babe?"

Malakai shrugged one large shoulder before tightening his hold around Murdoch and tucking him more firmly against him. "You are my *stella guida*, Murdoch. My guiding star." Capturing one of his vampire's thick locks between his thumb and forefinger, he rubbed the soft strands between them. "I will follow wherever you guide." Giving his lover a warm smile, Malakai added, "Besides, we'll find our way, raising your child or not."

Watching Murdoch nod, Malakai waited patiently for him to come to a decision.

Murdoch squeezed Malakai's thigh as he smiled at him, then turned his attention to Master Jaymes. "I guess that's decided. We'll have to meet with her to confirm Nester didn't knock her up." His voice tightened, but he pushed through it. "If he didn't, then we'd be happy to fulfill the contract."

"If she's pregnant," Malakai cut in. "Does that mean it's null and void?"

He would be the first to admit that he had no idea how such things worked.

When Murdoch hesitated to answer, Master Jaymes focused on the paperwork before him. He flipped from one page to the next. His gaze roved over them, telling Malakai that he was skimming them quickly.

Lifting his attention from the sheets, the vampire master smiled. "Yes. She has until mid-spring to fulfill her duties. If she's pregnant right now, she will not be able to give birth and become healthy enough to accept artificial insemination within that timeframe."

"Good enough." Murdoch shifted in his seat, his excitement evident. "I suppose we need to set up a meeting in neutral territory. She's under shifter protection, so somewhere west of Amarillo should work. Right?"

Master Jaymes turned his attention to Second Gypsum. "Arrange a meeting." Then he rose to his feet, Paul in his arms, indicating that the meeting was over. "I'll find out if Nester manipulated Lorain in some way."

"Oh." Paul slipped from Jaymes's arms and pulled open a drawer. He withdrew a pair of keys. He held them toward Murdoch. "You're in the third room of the green hall, at the moment." Cocking his head, Paul grinned cheekily as he focused on Malakai. "Sooooo, can I see your wings?" His expression turned quizzical. "Angels have wings, right? And halos?"

Malakai chuckled upon hearing Paul's innocent excitement. As Murdoch took the keys, Malakai told the human, "Yes, on the wings. No, on the halos."

Paul's eyes lit up. "Can I see?" he asked, appearing so eager.

Rubbing the back of his neck, Malakai glanced around the

room. Most of the ones in there were bonded. "It should be fine." Then he cleared his throat and explained, "The visage of an angel can be quite compelling to those not in a relationship, so uh . . . that's why I keep myself concealed. It's nothing to do with not trusting you all."

"Fair enough." Gypsum stepped over and rested a hand on Clarice's shoulder. With a wink, he told the female enforcer, "I'll keep you from throwing yourself at the angel."

Scoffing, Clarice rolled her eyes. "No offense, Malakai." She smirked at him while roving her gaze over him. "You're hot and all, but you're not really my type."

Malakai wasn't going to bother correcting her misconception—angels were *everyone's* type. With a thought, he released his glamour, revealing his true form.

There were a number of gasps and several startled *oh*s.

As Malakai peered around the room, he saw looks of appreciation, but the only sudden burst of arousal came from the unbonded Clarice. While she stared at him with covert appreciative glances, she crossed her arms over her chest and kept her place.

Impressed with Clarice's self-control, Malakai only waited several heartbeats. Then he returned his glamour into place.

"Wow," Paul murmured, his eyes wide. "You're definitely a hot guy." When Jaymes growled and frowned at Paul, his human laughed and peered at him through his lashes. "Oh, not as hot as you, big man, but you can't deny that Malakai's a good-lookin' fella."

"I don't need you pointing it out, though," Master Jaymes countered.

Humming, Paul shrugged one slender shoulder. "So, you don't want me pointing out his rugged good looks or those gorgeous wings I'd *love* to pet." His eyes narrowed a little bit more. "Or maybe how the highlights in his hair seem to catch the light just right or how his polo shirt molds to his—"

"Enough," Jaymes snarled, cutting off his beloved. "You're fixin' for a spanking, naughty beloved."

Paul rubbed his palms over his chest and murmured, "Promises, promises."

Growling, Master Jaymes grabbed Paul around the waist and swung him over his shoulder. He slapped one hand onto his human's ass, filling the room with a resounding smack. In response, Paul moaned and wriggled.

The scent of arousal flooded the office.

As Master Jaymes rounded his desk and strode toward the door, he stated, "Gypsum, let Mathe know I'll be an hour longer." Then the couple was gone.

A second later, several of the men in the room chuckled. They grinned and shook their heads. Even Clarice snickered as she headed toward the door.

Murdoch threaded his fingers through Malakai's, catching his attention. With a wink, he murmured, "That's normal for them."

Malakai nodded. "Paul did scent to be happy."

Laughing, Gypsum patted Malakai on his shoulder. "Paul loves to push Jaymes's buttons, and Jaymes loves that Paul stands up to him and does it." Shrugging, he wrapped his arm around Lucius's shoulders and began heading toward the door. "It works for them."

"Come on," Murdoch said, urging him to follow the others out of Master Jaymes's office. Once out of the room, his *stella guida* turned to the right. "We're in a room in one of the halls downstairs."

"Okay."

Malakai followed Murdoch through the sprawling, two-story ranch house. Making note of their turns, he made a mental map in his head. He had a perfect memory and had no desire to get lost due to inattention.

Once they reached a door in a hallway that was painted a

pale-green color, Malakai watched his vampire open the door. He followed his lover inside, locking the door behind him. Before he could even hope to take in his surroundings, he found his arms full of sexy, horny vampire who was kissing him within an inch of his life.

Perfect.

Humming appreciatively, Malakai was more than on board with anything Murdoch wanted to do — which turned out to be shower sex.

So much fun.

Chapter Eleven

On the way to their meeting with Lorain, a case of nerves flooded Murdoch. His angel was willing to raise his child. After Nester's betrayal, he'd mourned the loss of his missed opportunity, and now his angel was giving him that shot all over again.

What if Lorain is pregnant? What if Nester knocked her up? What would happen to the child?

Due to his actions, Nester had been remanded to the vampire council. A couple of enforcers had been to the coven just that morning. While, technically, Nester's crimes weren't grievous, Master Jaymes had decided Nester no longer had a place in his coven.

No one lied to his master's beloved.

Plus, Nester had indeed seduced Lorain. Although, from what Jaymes had told Murdoch and Malakai, it hadn't taken a whole lot to convince her. Evidently, she wasn't exactly the purest of women. Jaymes had learned that through the thoughts and memories Nester had delved into.

In fact, even the beta of the cougar shifter pride—Bradly Cooper—had had relations with Lorain.

Still, Doctor Sutherland had confirmed that Lorain wasn't pregnant during the course of their talks just a week prior to their contract being signed. A vampire would be able to tell almost immediately if that had changed. A pregnant woman began producing hCG—human Chorionic Gonadotropin. It changed the scent of her blood.

To that end, Second Gypsum had secured a meeting that

would include not only Master Jaymes, but Enforcer Clarice, Foreman Mathe, as well as themselves. They were supposed to be meeting with Alpha Forest, Beta Bradly, as well as Lorain and one of their enforcers. Doctor Sutherland was supposed to be there, too, as an impartial observer who'd been the witness to the signing of the contract.

When Foreman Mathe turned their SUV onto the paved road that led to a large picnic area and trailhead, Murdoch straightened in his seat. He glanced around quickly, waiting for the trees to break. Then they rounded a bend and Murdoch spotted three vehicles as well as a number of people sitting at a couple of picnic tables.

Murdoch saw Lorain sitting with Doctor Sutherland. The cougar shifters were seated at a different table. While he wondered if that meant something significant, he didn't make a comment.

"Are you ready for this?" Master Jaymes asked as Mathe parked their SUV.

Murdoch held back his snort. Instead, he claimed, "Yes, Master." When he saw the way his master arched one brow in silent question, he added, "As I'll ever be."

Jaymes smirked and dipped his chin in a slight nod. "We'll help get this sorted. Don't worry."

"And I'll be right beside you every step of the way," Malakai reminded him, pressing a kiss to Murdoch's temple. "We're a team."

Relief and pleasure filled Murdoch as he met his beloved's gorgeous aqua eyes. "Thank you."

"Anything for you, my *stella guida*."

Then Malakai took Murdoch's mouth in a claiming kiss. He didn't release him until someone cleared their throat, twice. By then, Murdoch panted for breath, and his cock ached where it pressed against his fly.

"Oh, yes. That's the impression you want to make," Mathe

teased with a laugh. "Let's go see your possible surrogate and her alpha with a hard-on."

Groaning, Murdoch felt his cheeks heat. He knew it was damn inappropriate, but any kiss from his beloved fired his blood, sending his need straight through the roof. In truth, Murdoch loved it, and he prayed that it would never change.

Still, at Mathe's teasing, Murdoch's arousal did wane a smidge. He could at least slide out of the SUV's back bench seat without strangling his dick. By the time he stood by the vehicle, waiting for Malakai to exit, his dick had gone down to half-mast.

Malakai threaded his fingers through Murdoch, and Murdoch smiled at his beloved. "Let's see what we can scent," Murdoch whispered.

After a nod from Malakai, Murdoch followed Mathe to where Jaymes, Clarice, and the shifters waited. He was quickly introduced to the alpha, beta, and the enforcer. Then Alpha Forest beckoned for Lorain to join them.

As soon as Lorain stood close enough, Murdoch scented it — the subtle change in the woman's scent. From the way the other vampires exchanged glances, he knew they had as well. Seeing Malakai's stoic expression, Murdoch knew he needed to share with his beloved.

She's pregnant.

Are you certain?

Murdoch had expected the question, and he nodded infinitesimally. *Afraid so.*

Any idea as to who the father is?

Inhaling deeply, Murdoch tried to parse out the tiny, *tiny* embryo growing within Lorain, that spark of life. He really needed to get closer, but since she'd stopped ten feet away, he didn't know a good way to do that.

"What do you mean the contract will be voided?" Alpha Forest demanded gruffly. "Lorain will either carry your vampire's child or your man will pay her what he owes."

77

"Lorain is already pregnant," Master Jaymes revealed. He tapped the side of his nose when Alpha Forest opened his mouth as if to counter. "A vampire can smell the changes in blood. It's how we choose who we'd prefer to feed from."

Snarling, Alpha Forest swung to face Lorain. "You whore," he roared. "You allowed yourself to get knocked up?" He growled as he curled his lip and pinned her with a disdainful stare. "Now you won't be able to pay your rent. I'm sure with the way you spread your legs, you won't have any problems living on the street."

"Wait a minute," Murdoch cut in, glancing between a far-too-pale Lorain to a clearly angry alpha. "You'd kick out someone from your pride just because she ended up pregnant?"

Alpha Forest scoffed. "I'm kicking her out because she can't pay her rent." Crossing his arms over his chest, he added, "Besides, she's *human*. Not really part of the pride. With her parents dead, there's no reason for us to keep taking care of dead weight."

Damn.

That was news to him.

"What if her child is a shifter?" Master Jaymes cut in. He pinned a cold gaze on Beta Bradly. "After all, the second has sweet-talked his way into her panties at least once." Narrowing his eyes, Jaymes growled, "Isn't that right, Beta?"

When Beta Bradly didn't answer fast enough, Alpha Forest demanded, "Is he speaking the truth, Brad?" He scowled at the big beta. "You bedded her?"

With his lip curled, he used a thumb to point at Lorain. After the beta jerked a nod, Forest glared at the enforcer, who'd been introduced simply as Simon. Simon quickly shook his head.

"Well, at least one of you knows how to keep it in your pants," Alpha Forest grumbled. He focused on Lorain and stated, "You have twenty-four hours to vacate your apartment. Don't make me send enforcers after you."

"Y-Y-Yes, alpha," Lorain squeaked. Her blue eyes were wide, and her body trembled.

Doctor Sutherland had his arm around Lorain, and he was glaring at the shifters, but he held his tongue.

Even as Alpha Forest began stalking toward his SUV, the beta and enforcer hesitated. They were obviously disconcerted by the alpha's decree, but they wouldn't meet anyone's gaze. They could barely even look at each other.

"Get moving, Brad. Simon," Alpha Forest roared. "I'm ready for dinner, and it's prime rib night."

"What if it *is* a shifter?" Bradly managed to find his tongue. He finally glanced Lorain's way. "I know we used a condom and all, but they fail. Could it be mine?"

Lorain's face turned beet red. Still, she found the courage to answer. "No, Beta Bradly. I had a test before signing the contract." Her voice finished on a whisper. "I-It's been too long."

"Oh."

Murdoch couldn't help but note how disappointed Bradly sounded. The shifter's shoulders slumped a little. After exchanging a glance with Simon, they both started toward the car.

With a sigh, Murdoch beckoned Lorain. When she frowned and stayed put. He urged, "Please, let me get a better scent of you. If you're carrying Nester's child, we need to know."

Lorain regarded Doctor Sutherland questioningly.

Doctor Sutherland nodded at Lorain. "It'll be fine, dear," he soothed. "One way or another. I won't allow you to be cast onto the street."

"Neither will I," Master Jaymes vowed, ignoring the rumble of the shifters' SUV. Once the vehicle left, the sound of the engine dying away, Jaymes continued, "For Nester's coercion, we do owe you restitution. We will be certain you and your child are well taken care of until you can stand on your own two feet. You are not alone."

The look of abject relief that crossed Lorain's face was damn near heartbreaking. She slowly moved toward them, her smile tremulous.

When Murdoch moved closer to Lorain, she tensed, staring at him with wide eyes.

"Please relax, Lorain," Murdoch crooned. "I would never hurt you." Carefully, he reached for her. After resting his hands on her shoulders, feeling the tension there, Murdoch assured, "I'll never bite you, so please try to relax. I just need to get a better scent of you."

Narrowing her eyes, Lorain questioned, "But you're a vampire. How can you promise you'll never bite?" Her cheeks flushed as she mumbled, "Not that it didn't feel great and all."

Smiling in understanding, Murdoch tipped his chin toward Malakai, who lingered a few feet away. "That's Malakai. I met him just a few days ago." Refocusing on Lorain, Murdoch told her, "Malakai is my beloved. Do you know what that means?"

Lorain's eyes widened, and her lips parted. Obvious understanding lit her blue-green eyes. "Oh. So you can only feed from him."

Murdoch nodded. "Exactly." Then he used a thumb to tip her chin up. "Now, let me scent you." Grimacing, he admitted, "With how many times I've fed from Nester, I'll know if you carry his child."

"Even at this early of development?" Lorain questioned, but she tipped her head back, baring her throat in an amazing display of trust.

"Even then," Murdoch confirmed.

Then Murdoch lowered his head and took a long inhale. He parsed out Lorain's natural flavor, recognizing her blood type as Nester's favorite.

No wonder he'd decided to seduce her. For some reason, his ex-lover never could resist seducing someone with AB-positive blood.

Should have known it then.

He was good at hiding his nature. Hearing Malakai's voice in his head, he glanced over his shoulder at his beloved. Malakai smiled at him, his gaze full of love. *And you'll never have to worry about his deceptions ever again.*

After nodding at Malakai just a smidge, Murdoch returned to his scenting of Lorain. He took a few more breaths. Then he found it—oh-so-faint and nearly hidden by Lorain's own blood, was the tissue signature of a tiny, growing life.

Straightening, Murdoch released Lorain and stepped backward. "You are carrying Nester's child."

"Shit," Lorain hissed. Her cheeks pinked even as she wrapped her arms around herself. "Even though I couldn't imagine who else it could have been, I was still hoping." Rolling a shoulder, Lorain blushed even darker as she peered at Doctor Sutherland. "Maybe hoping your test was wrong a couple of weeks ago."

"I'm sorry, my dear." The doctor offered her a kind smile. "But like these people said. You'll be taken care of."

Just as Lorain began to nod, a voice yelled, "I'm here to take what's mine!" That was followed up by several gunshots, which pinged off the nearby picnic table. "Give me Murdoch and Lorain, and no one has to get hurt."

CHAPTER TWELVE

Malakai felt a great wealth of sympathy for Lorain. While she obviously needed to learn to keep her legs shut, he sensed why she'd accepted so many lovers. Her parents had died a couple of years before, and she was desperately trying to find acceptance, companionship—even love.

In fact, Malakai had been so focused on Lorain and her pain that he had completely missed Nester's approach. Fortunately, now that he knew the man was there, he could easily do something about it.

"I need you all to cluster together," Malakai ordered softly. "I'll need you to restrain Doctor Sutherland and Lorain. Uh, maybe Clarice, too."

"What's your plan?" Master Jaymes asked, even as he discreetly signaled everyone to ease closer.

To Malakai's relief, Murdoch gripped Lorain's arm in one hand and Doctor Sutherland's in his other.

"I'm going to shield you from any more bullets," Malakai claimed, doing exactly as he'd claimed, erecting a magickal field around the others. "And now."

Malakai lowered his glamour.

Several gasps of appreciation sounded around the area.

"I'm totally not looking this time," Clarice grumbled. "Big, broad lug. Ugh, totally not my type."

"He's so handsome," Lorain murmured, awe and lust filling her voice. "Look at those wings. I need to touch. Let me go," she began to whine. "I need to touch, don't you see?"

"I see, my dear." Doctor Sutherland sounded equally entranced. "Such a gorgeous male specimen. I'm not gay, but I'd bend over for him. Gods, he's amazing."

Fighting back his urge to roll his eyes, Malakai focused on the single person he needed to enthrall. To his relief, Nester was staring right at him with hunger in his blue eyes. He parted his lips and licked them.

"Oh, you're so much prettier than Murdoch," Nester crooned, his expression predictably lust-drunk. "I can't wait to feel your ass." Lifting his free hand, Nester ordered, "You come here. I want you instead."

Perfect.

What are you doing?

Pretending to smile at Nester, Malakai sauntered toward Nester even as he mentally responded to Murdoch. *Relax, my* stella guida. *He cannot harm me. I have a personal shield up.*

A shield?

Malakai hummed through the line. *I can easily immobilize him, and your master can discover what happened to the enforcers that were escorting him.*

Damn, I didn't even think of that. I hope they're okay.

"You want me, Nester?" Malakai offered what he hoped was a flirty smirk at the vampire who'd obviously decided to go rogue. Turning a bit, Malakai ran his hand down his ass. "This is what you want?"

"Oh, yeah." Nester's breathing turned rough, and Malakai could see the outline of his erection in his jeans. Cupping that very same erection, Nester growled as he claimed, "Yeah, I'm gonna tear that ass up."

Malakai winked at Nester as he continued toward him. "What happens if I want your ass?" The words tasted like ash in his mouth, but he forced them out.

Nester curled his lip in a sneer. "I'm a top."

He's so not a top.

Upon hearing Murdoch's grumbled comment in his mind,

a wave of jealousy surged through Malakai. *My* stella guida, *please don't share your and Nester's sex life with me.* He couldn't help the hint of admonishment in his tone. In an attempt to soothe, Malakai added more. *I know you weren't a virgin when we met. That's not a vampire's nature, and I accept that. I just . . . I just don't want to hear about it.*

My apologies, my beloved. Just angry about this. No one should be dreaming of reaming your ass but me.

Mentally, Malakai hummed. *I will happily allow you to do that later, once we return to the ranch.*

Damn skippy.

Malakai arched one brow, uncertain what that meant.

Nester must have thought the move meant something else, for he leered as he claimed, "Don't worry, I'll be happy to prove it to you soon enough." Then he began reaching out, obviously intending to stroke Malakai's wing.

Yep. That's close enough.

Malakai reached out and grabbed Nester's wrist. He tugged and spun. With his other hand, he swept his arm upward, easily knocking the gun off trajectory. He ignored the bang, bang, knowing it couldn't hurt anyone.

Gripping that same wrist, Malakai squeezed a pressure point just hard enough to force Nester to drop the weapon. He swung Nester around and captured both of the vampire's hands behind his back with one hand. A quick kick sent the vampire's dropped weapon skittering into the trees.

A second later, Malakai spotted Murdoch at his side. "Are you injured?"

Shaking his head, Malakai assured, "I'm just fine, my star." In the next instant, he brought his glamour back into place. "It's safe," he called.

There was a reason Malakai didn't show himself to many. He didn't want to know what people wanted to do to him. To think that any non-bonded human or paranormal would attempt to have their way with him, and for the most part, he could read their thoughts, caused his stomach to churn.

"Good." Murdoch rested his hand on Malakai's arm. "Thank you, my beloved."

"Your beloved?" Nester snarled, peering over his shoulder at them. "What the fuck are you?"

Before Malakai could hope to answer, Nester grew his claws and swiped.

Pain surged through Malakai's fingers, and he jerked back in surprise.

Nester spun and lunged, his talons bearing toward Malakai's heart.

Growling, Malakai brought his wings round and spun, knocking Nestor off trajectory. He ducked and swept out his leg, taking out the rogue's feet. As the vampire fell, Malakai spotted the way he swung his arm, aiming for Murdoch's belly.

Malakai stepped between them, taking the stab. He groaned and stumbled backward.

Murdoch caught him, lending his support.

Master Jaymes appeared before Nester could gain his feet. The master slashed at Nester's belly, spilling his intestines all over the forest floor. As Nester grabbed at his stomach, Jaymes gripped the vampire's chin and forced his gaze up.

"Show me the memories of your escape," the master demanded.

Nester's expression went lax. His eyes grew vacant. His hands fell from his belly as he relaxed.

Seconds later, Jaymes released Nester's chin and straightened. Then he lopped the rogue's head from his shoulders.

Master Jaymes spun to face Malakai. His gaze roved over them both, his expression searching. "How is he?" he asked, obviously addressing Murdoch.

"I'm fine," Malakai assured, cutting in. "Already the pain ebbs."

"Seriously? You were just stabbed by a vampire's talons." Murdoch sounded disbelieving. "Let me see."

"I'm a doctor," Doctor Sutherland cried. "Let me past so I can help."

Turning his head, Malakai realized that Clarice was keeping Doctor Sutherland back. Mathe held a trembling Lorain. Everyone peered at him with fear and concern.

Warmth unlike anything Malakai had ever before experienced filled him.

Wow. So this is what it feels like to have . . . a family.

Malakai had always had the love of his creator, but he'd never had a family before.

Smiling, Malakai assured, "I'm truly going to be fine." He gripped the hem of his shirt and lifted, baring his stomach. Looking down, he spotted the dried blood and already healing gashes indicating where Nester's talons and entered and exited his body. "I heal far faster than anything you've seen before."

"Well, damn," Mathe muttered, his shock clear. "That's amazing." He grinned broadly. "Welcome to the coven."

"Wh-What are you?" the doctor asked in awe.

Clarice wrapped her arm around Doctor Sutherland's shoulders and quipped, "Congrats, Doc. You've just met your first angel." With a wink, she added, "FYI. If he ever decides to drop that glamour that hides his wings and aura, look away."

Doctor Sutherland's eyes widened as he nodded absently.

Blowing out a breath, Master Jaymes rumbled, "Well, I'm damn glad you're going to be okay, Malakai." He patted him on his shoulder even as he scowled and muttered, "Because I have a damn uncomfortable phone call to make to the council. They're going to have to retrieve the bodies of a couple of enforcers once I track them down."

Murdoch continued to hold Malakai even as he asked, "Nester killed them?"

Master Jaymes nodded once. "Yeah." Frowning, he added, "Their damn newbie tied Nester's hands behind his back, so when he freed himself from the cuffs, they didn't know it until it was too late."

"A definite change of procedures will be in order, then," Mathe grumbled even as he kicked Nester in the leg. "Asshole."

"Time to go home." Master Jaymes pointed at the body. "Grab that, will you, Mathe? Squish him behind the rear seat."

"Yes, Master." Mathe obeyed.

Malakai allowed his overprotective Murdoch to guide him toward the SUV. He smiled when his vampire called over his shoulder, "Will you follow us to the coven, Lorain? We'll get you set up in your new home."

Even as Lorain nodded, she whispered, "My baby's father is dead. He or she will never have one."

Malakai paused and focused on her, giving her a reassuring smile. "What that man was, was a sperm donor. He is nothing." Indicating himself and Murdoch, he declared, "While your babe won't have a father, per se, he will have uncles who care for him." Malakai noticed not only Murdoch's smile and nod, but every other vampires' as well. "Many, many uncles and aunts."

Lorain's breath hitched in her chest. She nodded tremulously. "Thank you." Leaning on Mathe, she allowed him to guide her to Doctor Sutherland's car.

Once she was safely inside, Malakai allowed Murdoch to help him onto the back bench seat of the SUV, even though he didn't need it. Cuddling his *stella guida* to his side, he nuzzled his nose against his vampire's temple.

"Now I know what you mean by spreading peace and love," Murdoch whispered into his ear. "Thank you."

Malakai met the warm gaze of his *stella guida*, happy to

have been able to give him something his heart desired. *Family.* "I'm looking forward to getting to my new home, too," Malakai admitted softly.

Murdoch leveled a serious look his way and said, "Where I will immediately take you to our suite's shower, clean you, and inspect every inch of your body."

Malakai smirked. "Every inch?"

His *stella guida's* eyes narrowed. "*Every* inch."

Malakai captured Murdoch's lips. Through his bond, he answered.

Sounds like the best plan to me.

ABOUT THE AUTHOR

Charlie started writing fantasy when she was eight, and after stumbling onto her first erotic romance at age nineteen, she realized her true calling. She now focuses on writing gay erotic romance, normally of the paranormal variety, with heroes of all kinds. With the help and support of her husband, Charlie finally fulfilled one of her life-long goals . . . move to acreage with her horses. You can often find her curled up with her laptop and a cup of tea or glass of wine, creating her next adventure. Charlie enjoys exploring the mountains of her new Oregon home on horseback, 4-wheeler, or motorcycle.

She can be reached at ch.richards2010@yahoo.com

Or visit her at www.charlie-richards.com.